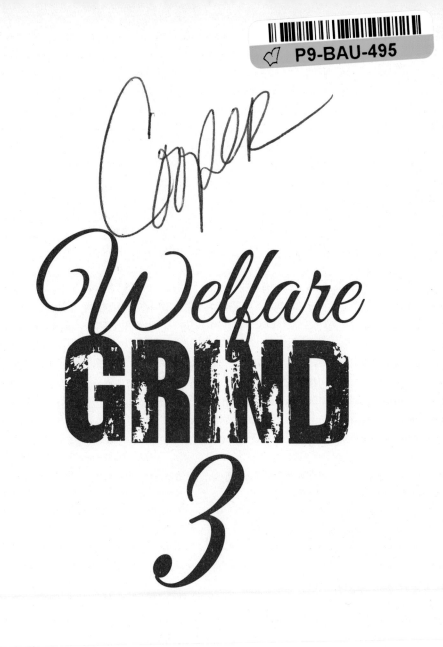

Welfare GRIND 3

KENDALL BANKS

Life Changing Books in conjunction with Power Play Media
Published by Life Changing Books
P.O. Box 423 Brandywine, MD 20613

Library of Congress Cataloging-in-Publication Data;

www.lifechangingbooks.net
13 Digit: 978-1934230633
10 Digit: 1-934230634

Acknowledgements

First and foremost, I would like to thank God. In the process of putting this book together, I realized how true this gift of writing is for me. He's given me the power to believe in my passion and pursue my dreams. I could never have done this without the faith I have in Him, the Almighty.

I once heard a rumor that some authors are opposed to expressing gratitude; that they feel if the gratitude is sincere; why not convey it directly to the person who deserves it instead of letting the whole world know. Well, since writing a book is never a solo effort, I couldn't disagree more.

From the bottom of my heart, I want to say thank you to all those who helped me along the way, and those who went the extra mile. My journey was a long, difficult road and without you, my goals would never have been fulfilled. From my publisher, Azarel who not only educated me about the writing process, but also made me a better writer, to the many test readers and editors who patiently and diligently proofread my drafts. A special thanks goes to all the LCB authors and Kellie, the best graphic designer in the business. I certainly appreciate your never ending support for me and LCB.

Lastly, to all the bookstores and readers who continuously purchase my books, I am truly indebted to you. Readers...you have no idea how grateful I am for your continued support and encouragement. Actually, it can never be appreciated enough. Your critiques (either good or bad) have helped mold my writing and made me aware of the endless possibilities I have when it comes to these characters. This has been the hardest book for me to write, so I truly hope that you enjoy it. Until the next time (book #7)...

Love,

Kendall Banks

Facebook: /authorkendallb
Twitter: @authorkendallb
Instagram: authorkendallb

Prologue

Never thought in a million years this moment would come. The hot slug from the .45 caliber gun had already ripped through my left thigh, yet I still managed to dig forcefully, fighting back the tears. Of course, I had to… or my ruthless attacker would shoot me again, this time at point blank range. My chest heaved up and down and my heart pounded each time the shovel entered the grainy dirt. Having to dig your own grave was more torture than the pistol staring me in the face.

Who even thought of such horrible bullshit? The small hole beneath me had taken me the last thirty minutes to dig and my attacker wanted it wider and deeper. The feeling of not knowing whether you'd be buried alive was heart wrenching. Suddenly, I began to wail. I couldn't hold out any longer. The next thing I knew the gun was pointed at the right side of my head. Then suddenly that dreadful cocking sound.

"And stop all that damn cryin'!" she spat.

I sniffled a bit, yet said nothing.

"Soldiers don't cry. You knew death was comin' your way. Now dig, or get your head splattered," she ordered.

I attempted to lift my arm slowly bringing the shovel back into position, only stopping after hearing a snicker. My killer's haunting laugh sent chills up and down my spine. Once again…torture. I didn't want to die. I wanted a second chance at life…to make things right. To say I'm sorry to all those I'd done wrong. So I asked, "Why?" in between my whimpers.

There was more laughter.

I stopped digging momentarily, even squinting from the pain in my leg.

"You know who got you here, right?"

I was confused. My expression showed it.

Then suddenly she appeared. All tied up and bloody I could see the pain in her eyes. She betrayed me, yet now we would die together.

I opened my eyes to speak when the first gunshot sounded. Then there was another…I just closed my eyes.

Chapter 1-

Treasure

With me, it's money over everything. I lived by those words. At an early age it was told to me that a broke nigga ain't good for shit. I mean, seriously, what's a broke nigga gonna do for me besides help me spend *my* money? That's what my mother would call straight hustling backwards. And hustling backwards never worked for me. Ain't got time for it. I deserved the best. That's why I decided to floss hard tonight. It's what I was accustomed to.

"HAPPY SWEET 16, TREASURE!" someone from the other side of the ballroom shouted.

The beautifully decorated room that had been completely transformed into a night in Paris made me grin widely. From the custom made red and black six-tier cake to the hired showgirls walking around with feather headpieces, lace corsets, and fishnet stockings. Everything accommodated the Moulin Rouge theme perfectly. I smiled even harder when my guest performer, 2 Chainz walked on stage and began performing his hit single, *Birthday Song*.

"All I want for my birthday is a big booty, hoe!" Everyone sang along.

Even Shane was having a ball as he danced off beat as usual. He clapped his hands so hard I knew they had to sting. He'd put on so much weight within the last few years, his small beer gut poked out from his shirt.

"Go Shane!" I yelled out. His crazy antics always found a way to make me smile.

I nodded my head and had a nice little weed induced buzz going as I stood in the center of the crowd draped on the arm of my man, knowing everyone around me wondered how I was able to get a famous rapper to come and perform at my party. Those who knew me well understood. A bitch like me was always used to getting what I wanted; even if it was the performance of a famous rapper.

Dressed in a black, sequin Alice & Olivia mini dress and my new studded Giuseppe platform booties, I was bossed the fuck up tonight. The price tag of my dress, shoes and jewelry was more than what most of my friends' parents made in a month working at their bum ass jobs. And if you factored in how much it cost to rent the Renaissance Hotel's ballroom at the Harbor and the two-toned Bentley Phantom that chauffeured me to the hotel's front door, it would only add insult to injury.

The entire room was filled nearly to capacity with so many people, I was hoping the fire marshall wouldn't come in and shut us down. All my friends and a large portion of my high school were in the house helping me celebrate, happy I'd invited them. All of them felt privileged, seeing as how I was the hottest chick in school. Without exaggeration, every bitch wanted to be me and every nigga wanted to be *with* me. But the role of being with me was reserved for just one nigga…

Rocco.

Although I was only sixteen, I'd snagged me one of the biggest heroin dealers in B-More. The nigga should've been nicknamed Frank Lucas from the movie *American Gangsta*, just because of the amount of shit he sold. The entire east side knew Rocco personally or had at least heard of him. Most people scattered when they saw him coming since his reputation for being that beast had spread across the city. He killed for fun and had been thrown into the grimey life at the age of ten.

Rocco was twenty-two years old; about six feet tall and had dreads that hung down to the center of his back. Along with sexy, root beer colored eyes, the nigga was tatted up just like Lil' Wayne. He was slim, but muscularly cut which blended perfectly with a wheat bread complexion. Everything else about him screamed, "That nigga." And to top it off, both his head skills and dick game were off the fucking meter.

"You good?" Rocco asked as he stood behind me dressed in a black Armani shirt and black jeans. His arms were wrapped tightly around me and his chin was over my shoulders as we stood among the crowd watching the performance.

"Yes, baby," I told him. "Everything's perfect. Whoever you paid to decorate the place did the damn thing." I looked around once again at the red and black décor, eyeing the feather centerpieces and candy apple favors. This shit could've easily been on an episode of MTV's, *Sweet 16*.

"Only the best for my baby," he told me in his raspy voice.

"The night has been perfect. From the five stacks you gave me, to the brand new Benz coupe, and the rented Bentley…it's all been more than I imagined," I said with an enormous grin.

"You sure you don't need nothin' else?" Rocco asked. "You need more money? Anything?"

Turning to face him, I placed my arms around his shoulders. "I'm good. I couldn't have asked for a better birthday party. I didn't know you had a soft side."

"I don't," he responded sharply. He then smiled giving me a chance to glare at his full lips and small gap between his teeth. The two of us kissed passionately, locking lips like they were glued together.

"Y'all hoes need to save that for the hotel room," my girl, Toya said playfully as she walked up on us. Everybody called her Toy for short.

I released my baby's lips and turned to see my friend standing in front of me in a sexy, red Herve Leger dress. Not many people could pull off the tight, body-hugging bandage dress, but Toy's curvy, eighteen-year-old figure filled it out perfectly. Among everyone in the ballroom, besides Rocco, Toy was the only person I trusted. She was my rock. We'd been hanging together since 8th grade even though she was two years older than me. She knew all about my troubled past and how I'd lived the life of bitches twice my age. I shared with her the times I had to smell the raw stench of blood. I cried on her shoulder countless times thinking about when I had to stare down the barrel of a gun, or when I had no choice but to pull one on my ratchet mother. Life had placed both me and Toy in similar situations, so we were meant to be best friends. We both had grown up all too fast; no time for tears, Barbie Dolls and Easy Bake ovens.

"What's good, girl? You look cute," I said, looking at her high, wildly styled bun.

"Thanks, but don't shit compare to this party. Damnnnnnnn," Toy said as if I should've already known. "This shit is hot! But how the hell did you get 2 Chainz to perform?"

I smiled slyly. "You know how I do."

"Well, however you did it got these bitches hatin'. You got 'em talkin', baby." Toy smiled, showing off her distinct cheek bones and heart-shaped face. With a light golden complexion, she was what most called a red-bone. "I even heard you got a C-class Benz today, so you know they're gonna be hatin' now!"

All I could do was smile.

Suddenly, Rocco's cell phone rang. He glanced at the screen and told me he'd be back in a minute. "This call is important."

He quickly excused himself. As he headed through the crowd, I noticed two broads standing at the entrance eyeing me. They'd been doing it all night, but I hadn't truly given any thought to it until I saw Rocco brush past them.

"You know them?" I asked Toy.

"Who?"

"Them bitches at the door." I turned to see venom in the eyes of the dark skinned chick with the nappy ponytail, rocking buckshots near the nape of her neck. "Don't turn around and look 'em in the face, Toy. Be discreet with the shit."

Toy turned and nonchalantly looked at the girls, then turned back to me. "I've seen the tall, dark-skinned chick around school, but they ain't nobody. Why, what's up?"

"They've been eyeballing me all night."

Toy shrugged her shoulders then stared them down for nearly thirty seconds. Before she could say anything, Rocco reappeared taking my attention away from my two stalkers. I started to ask him if he'd fucked one of them hoes, but he spoke bluntly, pissing me off.

"Treasure, look, I gotta make a run real quick."

"But you're gonna miss the presentation," I whined, showing my disappointment.

"Shhhhhhhh," he said, taking me in his arms and sticking his tongue down my throat forcefully. "I'm sorry, but I gotta handle this. I'm doin' this shit for us," he ended firmly before kissing me again.

I glared into his eyes realizing for the first time what people meant when they said he scares them with his eyes. It was like being hypnotized. He made you feel like you needed to obey, and quickly. Before I knew it, I agreed with him as he headed for the door. I was still disappointed though.

Moments later, 2 Chainz's performance was done and it was time for the surprise. As the DJ introduced me as the, "Birthday Girl" and invited me to the stage, the crowd parted like the Red Sea; like the queen was coming through. Once I hit the stage and grabbed the mic, all eyes were on me. Surely they wondered if another celebrity like Drake or Big Sean were coming out next. Staring out into the crowd, I felt like a rock star, like Beyonce or some shit. I felt the urge to break out into a song and dance.

"Y'all having a good time?" I asked loudly, hearing my voice echo.

The crowd came alive.

"Well, make some noise out there then!"

The crowd erupted even louder.

"That's what I'm talking about! Thanks for coming out to help me celebrate my Sweet 16!"

The crowd cheered even more.

"I appreciate all of you coming, but this isn't just my night, though. This night belongs to someone close to my heart. If it wasn't for her, I wouldn't be here."

Everyone watched me, wondering who I was talking about.

"I want y'all to give it up for the number one woman in my life! My mother!" *Damn, it hurt me to lie like that, but I knew she needed to hear it.*

The ballroom erupted in cheer as my mother was wheeled onto the stage. She was dressed in a long, red Michael Kors wrap dress and her natural hair was draped beautifully across her shoulders. Although confined to a wheelchair, she was still the strongest woman I'd ever met. And she definitely had crazy will-power. At this point I was starting to think her ass had nine lives; this time surviving like 50 Cent. I don't know if I could've come back the way she did after being shot once again…three times. I don't think I could've accepted it.

It had been four years since my mother had taken those bullets from Frenchie on the sidewalk and lost her ability to walk. She'd been paralyzed from the waist down ever since. Yet she never stopped fighting to get better. My mother smiled as I gave her a huge hug followed by a peck on the cheek. Moments later, I looked back out over the ballroom.

"This is the strongest woman I know, y'all!"

The crowd erupted in cheer again, this time so loudly my mother cried.

"Keema! My Keema!" Shane yelled out. Once again, he clapped his hands wildly.

"I've got something special for you," I said to her.

Moments later, Toy pushed out a brand new wheelchair on stage which I'd spent a few thousand to customize. Everything on it was electronic. It was specially painted in a beautiful platinum color, and also came equipped with a cell phone, radio and several other high-tech gadgets.

Even though my mother smiled, I could tell something was off. I'd seen that look before, but tonight I ignored it. Maybe I was just reading too much into it. Besides, the night was going too good to let anything mess it up. As the crowd continued to cheer, two of my homies lifted my mom from the old chair she was in and placed her into the new one. After instructing the DJ to crank up the music, I then wheeled her off the stage.

I knelt in front of my mother and asked proudly, "Do you like it?"

She paused for a second.

Something was wrong.

"Ma, what's up?"

"How much did you pay for this chair, Treasure?"

"A couple stacks. Why?"

"Look, I don't mean to sound ungrateful, but there are other things you could've contributed that much money to. You know what I'm talking about."

I sighed, knowing where this was going.

I fumed inside. Now was not the time to battle complaints.

"I'm gonna get you the money," I finally said.

"When?" she badgered.

I sighed again and rolled my eyes. "Soon."

"You always say that, Treasure. You've been saying that for over a year now, and I'm tired of it. I'm tired of depending on people."

"Ma, come on. Let's not talk about this tonight."

"Why not?"

"Because it's my birthday, and I'm trying to celebrate, that's why!" She was starting to press my buttons.

"I'm sick of you shrugging this off likes it's nothing…like it's minor! I need that money, not a damn wheel-chair."

That was it. I snapped.

"You ungrateful bitch! I go out of my way to do some-thing nice for you and all you can think about is yourself! I share my night with you and all you can do is complain! Have you looked at yourself in the mirror? You haven't looked this pretty in years, and it's all because of me."

"Treasure, it's not like…"

"Fuck that! I don't wanna hear it."

Unable to face her anymore, I left my mother by herself and stormed off to the bathroom. I needed to be alone for a minute. I'd most likely go back out and apologize to her, but for now I had to get myself together. Dealing with my mother since the accident hadn't been a walk in the park. With all her mood swings, whining, crying, complaining, cursing and "Whoaaa is Me" attitude, the bitch was really beginning to do the Stanky Leg on my damn nerves; chipping away at my sanity. She was like medication. I could only deal with her in doses. Too much of her drove me fucking crazy. I needed weed to help me cope.

I'd gotten the habit honestly. My mother smoked weed for as long as I could remember. She always had me and my brothers around it. Every time she was going through some-thing, she smoked. Even when she *wasn't* going through some-thing she smoked. So, I guess it was only natural that it would rub off on me.

I walked into the bathroom, found the furthest stall from the door and went inside. After closing the door and sliding the latch, I sat down on the toilet, reached into my purse and pulled out a blunt. Opening my thighs a little, I split the blunt with my fingernails and emptied its stuffing into the toilet. Seconds later, I filled it with weed, tightened it up and blazed.

After inhaling deep, its smoke comforted my lungs and gave my head an enjoyable cloudy feeling. Moments later, I released it. Through heavy hanging eyelids I watched the smoke leave my lips and slither towards the ceiling until my cell phone rang.

Glancing down at the number, I answered with a devious grin. "You got that money you owe me," I said, already knowing exactly what the call was about.

"What type of games are you playin'?" he screamed into the phone. "Why the fuck would you post naked pictures of me all over the grounds of my son's school? Are you crazy? They showed my face!"

I smiled, taking another hit of the blunt. "Pictures of your dick being posted at your son's school are the least of your worries. If you don't pay me what you owe, the video of you fucking my underage friend is going straight to the police."

"What?"

"You heard me, Vegas. I doubt if you wanna add sex offender to your criminal record, so I strongly suggest that you pay up. Besides, the pictures were posted because you're one week past the due date muthfucka."

"You sneaky, connivin' bitch!"

After exhaling the smoke to the ceiling again and laughing, I told him, "I may be a bitch, but you're a freaky ass thirty-eight year old man. You should be ashamed of yourself for all those nasty things you had her doing to you. You know sex offenders can't go within a thousand feet of a school."

"Damn it, Treasure!"

I knew I was playing with fire since Vegas had a troubled past. He was a former big time drug dealer trying to live the straight life; family and all. But money prevailed. He fucked up and now he had to pay. "Twenty thousand, Vegas. Twenty thousand dollars and all this goes away like it never happened."

"You know I don't have no fuckin' twenty thousand dollars. I work like a regular Joe now. You know I changed my life. I told you that shit!"

"Yeah whatever, I don't believe that shit. I know you still got money stashed away somewhere. Y'all niggas live in Glen Burnie, and you still drive a nice ass Audi. You need to figure out how to get my cash. I don't care how you do it. Just do it."

"You triflin' bitch, this is not what we agreed on at first! We agreed on *one* night! I paid you for that night! This shit ain't fair!" Vegas belted.

"*Life* aint fair, nigga. You know that."

"I'm gonna kill you, bitch! Do you hear me? I'm gonna kill you!"

"Yeah, yeah, yeah, whatever. Just get my money. You've got one more week."

With that said, I hit the end button and tossed the phone into my purse, not worried about his threats. They always made threats. However, since my victims knew there were more copies of the videos and pics than just the ones in my possession, they always realized the best thing to do was pay up.

I rubbed my hands together hastily, thinking about how my cash was stacking up.

Chapter 2-
Keema

The bright orange rays of the early morning sun blazed through the curtains of my bedroom window as I lay in bed. An episode of *Judge Judy* played on the television, but at low volume. I wasn't watching it, though. It was pretty much watching me as I laid in my nightgown staring mindlessly into a distance while clutching a tall glass of vodka in one hand and multiple pills in the other.

Twenty-eight to be exact.

Eighteen sleeping pills and ten antidepressants.

In my lap was an ash tray and on the nightstand was the bottle of Peach Ciroc I'd been working on for the past hour.

Most people started their morning off with a plate of scrambled eggs and sausage, not a drink and certainly not enough pills to kill themselves with. But most people weren't fucking cripples like me. They had no idea what it was like to be damn near helpless. I used to start my day off happily and woke up with a bright smile on my face. Now, I barely smile at all, and when I did it felt stiff and awkward. I also prayed to God every night hoping not to wake up at all. Shit, I was so fed up with my situation I wished those bullets I took four years ago would've just killed me. That would've been a lot easier.

Right after Frenchie and Shy left me on that sidewalk bleeding that dreadful day, both of them disappeared into thin fucking air with the inheritance check. No one's heard or seen them since, not even the police. I assumed they were still fugitives since the police hadn't come by to tell me otherwise. Those muthafuckas were probably hiding out in another country by now; sipping on daiquiris every day. Either way, they'd definitely left their mark…directly on my fucking spinal cord. After being shot three times, one bullet shattered the left side of my rib cage, while the other two made a b-line straight to my spine, severing every nerve.

I'd been in and out of the hospital countless times over the past four years, damaging my need for life…my will to live. To say paralysis is a bitch was an understatement. The days of being able to tell if something was sharp, soft, hot or cold were long gone. The only thing I could feel below my waist was the pressure of someone touching me. The only thing I looked forward to now and had grown an addiction for were my pills, alcohol and cigarettes. Those bastards had really fucked me up.

The past four years of my life were only filled with doctors, medication, rehabilitation, disappointment and heartbreak. I missed the days when I used to be able to get the fuck up and go about my business when I wanted to.

I missed driving.
I missed being able to walk into a store.
I missed my independence.
I missed having good, nasty sex.
I missed grinding.
I missed my damn life!

If that shit wasn't bad enough, I was still on probation from being charged with several counts of identity theft and fraud a few years ago. Right after I was shot, I was eventually charged for the welfare scheme when my court case came around. But fortunately due to my severe injury, the lawyer that Lucky hired for me kept postponing the court date. I stayed in the hospital so long I couldn't even make it to court. When he couldn't postpone it anymore, my lawyer eventually entered in a guilty plea due to the evidence against me. However, instead of serving any prison time, the judge agreed to a long, four year probation. Maybe the judge felt sorry for my crippled ass. Maybe he thought that by me being paralyzed, I could do no more harm. But I would've served several years in prison if that meant I could have the use of my legs again.

With a much laid back probation officer who only frequently checked up on me the first year, he'd made my probation period a breeze. He only called or stopped by now once every two or three months. I only had a few more months left to go, and couldn't wait until I was finally off those papers.

Suddenly, I looked over at the wheelchair beside my bed. The damn thing seemed to taunt me. It turned my stomach and angered me so much I wished I could get up and sling it across the room. It was the tackiest thing I'd ever seen in my entire life. I mean, who the hell ever heard of putting spinners on a fucking wheelchair? Who does that? Although it was supposed to be a gift to cheer me up, all it did was depress me even more. All it did was remind me of what I couldn't have…

The use of my legs.

This wasn't the life I was used to, and I couldn't hold on any longer. I was tired of trying to appear normal; wanting to be enthusiastic, but instead feeling like lead. I was tired of thinking about every failure, every bad experience, and every fuck up. The feeling of no longer wanting to exist had done me in. All I wanted to do was cry, but there were no more tears left. Besides, sobbing would take effort, which I no longer had.

I constantly asked myself, why I should continue to fight the pain of depression. But since I couldn't come up with a reasonable answer, killing myself seemed like the best option. Yeah, I was definitely taking the punk way out, and I knew this would hurt the people who cared about me, but none of that mattered anymore. I was convinced that they would be better off without me anyway. Besides, no one understood what the fuck I was going through. It was finally time to give up.

At that moment, my cell phone rang from the nightstand, causing me to sigh. I didn't want to talk to anyone at a time like this. Anytime someone called, their voice always sounded like they felt sorry for me, like I was a damn charity case. However, this time I decided to answer after realizing the ringtone belonged to Lucky. I guess if I had to talk to someone before I ended it all, it might as well be him.

I placed the glass down on the nightstand and grabbed my phone. "Hello."

"What's good, Keema?"

"Nothing," I answered in a somber tone.

"I'm callin' to see how you've been. You takin' care of yourself?"

"Yeah," I lied.

Over the past four years, Lucky had been a sweetheart; both him and Ms. Kyle. Lucky in particular always got to Baltimore as often as he could to check up on me, Treasure and Shane. He'd stay for weeks, waiting on me hand and foot. The only disappointing thing about it was that he still wasn't ready to test the waters with me in a relationship again. Sometimes I wondered if it was because I was crippled and because I would probably never be able to fuck him real good again. He hadn't even made it back to Baltimore in almost six months, so I was definitely into my feelings about that.

"How was the party last night?"

"It was alright," I said dryly.

"Just *alright*? I thought it was supposed to be some type of fly, T.V. type shit. That's what Treasure told me every time I called. Damn, I hate I missed it, but I got a lot of good things in the works out here in Phoenix. Real good things."

He better not be talking about another bitch, I thought.

Annoyance filled me. Remembering the party only made me glare at that tacky ass wheelchair; and seeing that shit only reminded me that I was fucking handicapped.

"Look, Lucky, the party was alright, okay? I really don't wanna talk about it."

"Keema, what's up? Something's wrong. Talk to me. What's goin' on?"

With a sigh, I closed my eyes. I wanted to tell him how much I needed him, how much I wished he would forgive me for causing him to get shot up years ago. I wanted to tell him how badly I wanted to make love to him. There was so much I wanted to say and needed to say, but now it was pointless.

"It's nothing, Lucky. Look, I'm glad you called. Now, I get a chance to say that I love you; always have and always will. Please don't be mad, but I need peace and today I'm going to get it."

"What's that supposed to..." Lucky said, just before I hung up the phone and powered it off.

At that moment, I picked up the glass then placed a handful of pills in my mouth. After washing them down with the warm vodka, I continued the process until all the pills were gone. Satisfied with my choice, I felt the corners of my mouth turn up, producing somewhat of a smile. I was finally happy. Suicide seemed to welcome relief, and that's exactly what I needed.

Just as I opened my mouth to drink the rest of the alcohol, my bedroom door swung open and Treasure switched inside. She glared at me and the glass in my hand disapprovingly. Knowing it annoyed the shit out of her to see me like this, I took the last heavy gulp right in front of her. Shit, I didn't even have time to write a suicide note.

Treasure just shook her head, folded her arms over her breasts and leaned back against the wall looking just like me these days; with the exception of the piercing on her bottom lip. Each day we were beginning to look more like twins. Gone was the skinny little knock-kneed girl she'd once been. Treasure was now growing into womanhood with a nice, round ass and hips to match. Her style was also on point. Keeping her twenty-six inch Brazilian weave and nails freshly done, she also dressed like a runway fashion model. We'd definitely switched places. Now, I was the frail bitch with no appetite, no confidence and no self-esteem.

"Is this all you want to do all day? Just drink yourself to death?"

"Can you think of something better for me to do?"

"Yeah, as a matter of fact, you can try getting out of that bed, getting dressed and getting some damn exercise. It's the first day of fall and it's gorgeous outside."

I rolled my eyes. I wasn't trying to hear that shit. Why the fuck would I want to go outside? What, to see some fucking leaves changing colors? Besides, once I got out there, people would just stare at me and whisper, labeling me as a cripple. They would probably even videotape me with their cell phones, uploading that shit to YouTube and having me all over the internet. I'd look like a damn fool.

"Nah, I'll pass."

"So, you're just gonna keep feeling sorry for yourself?" she asked.

I ignored her.

"Ma, I don't know what you want from me. I tried to make you happy last night by sharing my night with you."

"Make me happy?" I questioned in disbelief.

"Yeah, make you happy. And all you did was embarrass me."

"I embarrassed *you*? So, you buy me a cheesy-ass wheelchair and then have the nerve to say *I* embarrassed *you*. Treasure, *you* made *me* look like a damn sideshow freak last night. I already have an electronic chair, and didn't need another one. You know I could use money right now!" I could feel myself becoming weaker by the minute.

"I thought you would like the new chair. I wanted you to have the best. You really need to be thankful that I'm here for you. It ain't like people are beating down the door to help you."

That comment stung. Badly. "What did you say, girl?"

"You should be happy you even have people left in your life," she fired back. "You got Ms. Kyle taking care of Deniro and you got me taking care of Shane and all of the bills. So, be grateful!"

"No, *you* need to be grateful," I spat. "Don't act like I've never been there for you. Oh, so because I can't walk, now you suddenly have amnesia? Let's not get shit twisted, Treasure. I taught you all about these fucking streets. I taught you how to hustle. And let's not forget, I even taught you how to get the fake ID's so we can get some welfare money coming up in here. Speaking of that, why haven't you done it yet? That's free money that you're turning your nose up at."

Treasure glared at me evilly. "Oh, so we're keeping count of how many times we've been there for each other now? Besides, I could care less about that bullshit ass welfare money. It's not even worth my time. The amount of cash I make doing my other gigs, makes that shit look like pennies." She paused. "I mean, why are you always talking about welfare? Didn't you learn your lesson after getting locked up? You're still on probation now for that shit. If you haven't noticed, I'm trying to break the cycle."

"Treasure, don't get cute. I took care of you and your brothers with that so called bullshit money. We didn't have to struggle because of that money."

"And now I take care of you with *my money*. I pay all the bills and I buy all the food, so the days of you running shit around here are long gone." She shook her head. "You can't even reach the cereal on the top shelf, so I advise you to stay in your lane."

"That's low, Treasure. I taught your fucking ass everything you know."

"Do you really want to go there with me? I don't think you do because you'll only get your damn feelings hurt."

I felt myself nod as Treasure continued to rant. I had to hit her with something major.

"Well, don't forget the fact that I've kept your secret all this time."

We both remained silent for seconds, her eyes staring me down with anger. She hated when I had one up on her. I knew that comment would sting.

"Do you want us to start playing tit for tat?" she finally asked, her chest heaving up and down. "Not only that...do you want me to talk about all the times we had to skip town and run from niggas because of *your* bullshit? Do you want me to tell you what type of mother you were? Do you want us to talk about Imani, Cash and Grandma, huh? Is that what the fuck you want to do? Because if it is, let's get to it."

All I could do was sit and seethe in fury. My daughter was heated, but she was right. I definitely didn't want to go there. I'd brought hell to our doorstep far too many times. It was because of me that my mother, best friend and youngest child were dead. The last thing I wanted to do was discuss it. I felt bad enough as it is.

"Yeah, I didn't think so," Treasure replied. "I haven't forgotten about all the shit you made me witness and be a part of over the damn years. I haven't forgotten all the shit I was *forced* to learn."

I felt myself nodding once again, as a bit of dizziness appeared.

"Well, if you've learned anything from me, the most important is that you need to always watch your back, Treasure. As long as you're fooling with the streets and niggas in the streets, karma will eventually catch up with you. It's the nature of the beast. The shit doesn't stop. It just goes on and on until you find yourself laid up like me."

Treasure exhaled hard, not wanting to hear it. As usual, her ass thought she knew every damn thing there was to know about life. Seeing her react like that towards my advice about the game annoyed the shit out of me. Treasure reminded me of myself in so many ways. She thought she was Super Woman, just like I did, just before Frenchie put those three bullets through my body.

"Well, I'm not gonna end up like you, trust me," Treasure replied.

"I-I-I-I-I just want you you you to l-e-a-r-n frommmm my mistakes," I stuttered. This time I struggled to get the words out. It felt like my head weighed a ton as I fought to hold it up.

"And what's wrong with you?" she asked suspiciously. "Are you drunk? You know you're not supposed to be drinking with all the medication you're on. How many times do I have to tell you that?"

As Treasure continued to rant, I could hear her talking, but couldn't make out exactly what she said. I felt completely disoriented. At that point, I tried to open my mouth to respond, but nothing would come out. Within seconds, it felt like someone was strangling me, cutting off my airway as I struggled to breathe. Next, came shockwaves of pains in my chest and it felt as if my heart was about to explode. All I could remember before blacking out was my body shaking uncontrollably, going into some type of convulsion. I'd finally gotten what I wanted.

Death.

Chapter 3-

Keema

    The curtains were closed and the room was silent, giving it a gloomy and depressing look and feel. The only sound was the constant beeping of the IV machine beside me and the voice of a nurse coming over the intercom system in the hallway occasionally. As the machine beeped, my veins felt cold while the thin tube fed them with fluid. I lay in the bed on my back underneath crispy white sheets with my face turned towards the stark white wall. Miserable beyond belief, I didn't want to talk to anyone. I wished I'd been successful last night.

    I wished I was dead!

    My nose was still sore and I had a slight headache from the long, plastic tube the doctor had shoved into it last night to pump my stomach. It was one of the most humiliating moments of my life. It was also one of the most painful. The pain from the tube was unbearable and made me gag so much that I had to be strapped down by my wrists. On top of that, it still felt like I wanted to gag. My stomach hurt like hell, and I had a terrible taste in my mouth from some black shit they gave me to induce vomiting. The entire experience was horrific!

"I'm glad to see you awake, Ms. Newell," a doctor said as he stood at the foot of my bed with a clipboard tucked underneath his arm. I was in such a daze that I hadn't heard him come in. "I just came to see how you're feeling."

I turned to face him. "I've had better days." My throat felt like it was on fire and I was extremely hoarse.

"Ms. Newell, due to the amount of pills you ingested, and due to your liver being able to detect an early stage of disease, I ran a blood test last night, and thankfully the results came back negative. However, that doesn't mean you're out of the woods yet. Although your liver is still functioning well, the abdominal pain you might be experiencing is because of some form of damage. Ms. Newell, do you understand that if this happens again, the severity of the medication can cause complete liver disease? Do you understand how serious that is?"

I only nodded my head.

"Why do you keep doing this to yourself? He checked my chart. "This is the second time you've attempted suicide in just a one year period."

My eyes immediately dropped to the scar across my right wrist. It was several months old. I'd slit my wrist in the bath tub one day after being in a severely depressed mood. If Treasure hadn't found me, and rushed me to the hospital, I would've surely successfully bled to death.

"I know this is the second time," I finally spoke. "I can count. Why do you think I keep doing it? Why does anyone do it? Isn't it obvious? I wanna die, stupid. Who the fuck let you graduate from medical school?"

I went back to looking at the wall as the doctor folded his arms across his chest and sighed. I was absolutely fed up. Seeing another day on earth without the use of my legs was intolerable. My strength was gone. My will to fight had evaporated. There was nothing left but memories and regret. I dreaded them both. They burned like fire, ate through to my core like acid and cut as deeply as knives. Who the hell could take day after day of that? I sure couldn't.

"Ms. Newell, I understand how you're feeling but this isn't…"

I turned away from the wall, locking my eyes on him fiercely. "How the fuck do you understand how I feel? You can walk!" I screamed. I was tired of people saying those words to me. They had no fucking idea whatsoever what it was like to be me.

Hearing me yell, a nurse suddenly peeked inside the room. With a young, baby doll face, it looked like she was a college student or at least in her early twenties. "Is everything okay, Dr. Tatum?" she asked, stepping inside.

He nodded to her. "Ms. Newell, you can't give up hope."

"Doc, the only hope I have is that my daughter finally gives me the money I need to get a stem cell operation so I can walk again." The doctor looked confused. "Yeah, I'm sure you've heard about it. I've read and researched about this surgery for a year now. It's still not legal in the U.S., but I don't care."

"Ms. Newell, even though stem cell isn't my expertise, I wouldn't recommend that you go forward with any surgery that hasn't been approved yet. That's too much of a risk, and no, I've never heard of the surgery."

"Well, it's a risk I'm willing to take. You wanna know *why*, doc?"

He didn't answer. He and the nurse just stared at me crazily.

"Because I'm not gonna live the rest of my fucking life being a cripple, that's why. And since it's obvious that I'm never successful with killing myself, I'm going to get that seventy-five grand, and I'm taking my ass over to the Dominican Republic to get that surgery. You see my glimmer of hope comes with an expensive price tag."

Obviously, since I was in no shape to get out and hustle,

I had to depend on Treasure. But for the past year, she'd been slow poking around on getting the money up; telling me over and over again that it would happen soon. She'd yet to come through. All I needed was at least a deposit of twenty-five grand to get the ball rolling, and she hadn't even done that.

Neither the doctor nor the nurse said a word as I rolled over and zoomed back in on the wall. Looking at it was much more interesting than looking at them.

"I see you're still just as unappreciative as ever," Treasure's voice sounded.

I turned to see her standing at the door with Rocco.

"Don't mind her, doctor," Treasure said to him. "She's this grumpy with everybody."

"It's okay," he responded. "I understand. I'll leave you guys to talk."

He walked out of the room while the nurse pushed a few buttons on my IV machine.

"What do you want?" I asked Treasure dryly.

"To make sure you're okay, and to bring you this," she said, placing my purse on one of the chairs in my room. "Your phone is inside and fully charged."

I rolled my eyes and looked at the wall again.

"You really are a miserable bitch," Treasure sassed.

I turned to her.

"Chill, Treasure," Rocco said.

"Nah, fuck that. I saved her life for the damn umpteenth time and I can't even get a thank you from her."

"Did I ask you to save my life, Treasure, huh? Has it ever occurred to you that maybe I don't want to be here? Has it?"

"Well, has it occurred to you that maybe your feelings and what you want aren't the only things that matter? Other people care about you. Lucky has been worried sick since you hung up on him. He's been calling me all day."

"Well, if you and Lucky care so much, why am I in this

bed right now, Treasure, huh? Why am I not walking?"

"Now, I understand why Lucky hasn't been back here in a while. Now, I understand why he's getting married," Treasure blurted out.

The size of my eyes become two times larger. "Married…what the hell are you talking about?"

"Oh, he still hasn't told you yet?" Treasure questioned. "I mean…I hope you didn't think he wasn't gonna move on with his life."

So, that's the 'good things' he was talking about, I thought. *Out of all the times we'd talked, I can't believe his ass had failed to mention that shit.*

"Treasure, I need for you to leave. I'm not in the mood for visitors right now," I ordered.

With those words said I glanced at Rocco who had a bland, stony look on his face. I hated that about him. He had an air about him that always made me feel uncomfortable. I wanted his money though, so I never said anything to him about my thoughts. I looked back at the wall.

Treasure knew what my glance meant. That son of a bitch she was with drove multiple high priced cars. He rocked no less than a hundred thousand dollars worth of jewelry at any given time. His outfits were Gucci and nearly every other high end designer in existence, and he always kept a fat knot in his pocket. The nigga had money to burn. The fact that he was a twenty-two year old man practically molesting my baby meant nothing to me. I was desperate. He had something I needed. And if it meant letting him bang Treasure's sixteen-year-old pussy out to get it, so be it. Who cares if he was a damn pedophile? As long as he paid for my surgery, that's all I cared about. All Treasure had to do was ask him for the money; he'd give it to her. Then again, she could take it. She kept stacks of his money in our house all the time; holding onto it until he picked it back up. The thoughts of it all made me sick again. Shit, if her ass couldn't handle him, then she needed to pass him over to me.

"Ms. Newell, I'm glad you're straight," Rocco told me as he took a seat. "If you need anything while you're in here, don't be afraid to ask me."

"Don't call me that like I'm an old ass lady. My name is Keema," I snapped while admiring the icy jewels around his neck. I looked back at Treasure, who was now by the window carrying on some sort of conversation with the nurse.

"Can you call Deniro for me? I wanna talk to him." I asked her.

"Why, so he can discover his mother doesn't love him enough to keep from cutting her wrists and shoving pills down her damn throat?" Treasure fired back.

My eyes narrowed in spite at her. It was another low blow. But it was the truth.

Six months after getting shot, I allowed Ms. Kyle to take Deniro and move to Hampton, VA. As difficult as the decision was, I knew it was the best thing for my son at the time. I wasn't able to take care of him properly, so it was only right that I agreed to let someone who I considered a mother figure step into his life and takeover. Someone with a positive influence and protective energy who could help place him in a better environment. It started off as a temporary agreement until I was able to get back on track.

But when Ms. Kyle realized that I'd sank into a deep depression, that brief arrangement obviously turned into long-term. That wasn't a bad thing though since Deniro needed to be as far away from Baltimore as possible. Hell, we all did. But Treasure vowed to never leave the city. Being that my daughter had already gone through so much in her young life, I decided not to press the issue. I also decided to stay in Baltimore to look after her as best I could. In my mind, that was my way of trying to start over and be a good mother. But looking at the way things were going, guess I hadn't done such a good job.

"You need to go get Deniro," Treasure added.

I shook my head. "You know I'm still not in a position to take care of Deniro, Treasure. He's better off with Ms. Kyle right now. Plus, he loves it in Virginia. He tells me that every time I talk to him."

"So what. He needs to be with his mother. Not some lady pretending to be."

"Look, just like Lucky helped me take care of you and Shane when I first got shot, I need Ms. Kyle's help now. Sorry you don't agree, but the last time I checked, I didn't need your opinion about my child."

"Well, if you stop trying to kill yourself every other week, I wouldn't have to give you my opinion," Treasure spat.

"Yo', that's enough," Rocco butted in.

Instead of giving him attitude, Treasure just rolled her eyes and turned back towards the nurse. As they spoke, I leaned towards them to ear hustle. Knowing my daughter, I listened carefully. Treasure was trying to keep her tone low, possibly to keep me from hearing, but I recognized exactly what she was doing.

Treasure was casual as she asked the nurse her name and age. She tried to act like they were just having a casual conversation, as if there was no interest, but I knew better. I knew exactly what she was doing.

She was sizing the nurse up.

"Ay, Treasure," Rocco said, looking at his iced-out Royal Oak Audemars watch. "I got that thing to handle."

His voice was stern. Too stern. I didn't like the idea of him controlling my child.

"I know," she told him. "Give me a minute."

"Make it quick. They from out of town, so they don't like to wait too long."

"I got you," she assured.

With that said, Treasure went back to her conversation. It was time for her to sink her teeth into the unsuspecting nurse just like she'd done to every other young naive girl she'd recruited to be a part of her hustle.

"I know a part time job you would be perfect at," Treasure said, pulling a wad of money from her purse.

"No, Treasure," I interrupted.

"Ma, this ain't got nothing to do with you," she said without looking at me.

"This is my hospital room, so it has everything to do with me."

The nurse looked confused as her eyes went back and forth from me to Treasure and then the money.

Treasure flipped her hand at me and went back to talking to the nurse.

"I'm serious, Treasure," I told her louder than before. "I mean it. Don't make me hit the button on the side of this bed and have somebody call the police. I'll tell them exactly what you're in here doing. Besides, if you don't come up off of my surgery money, I'm blowing up your little scheme."

Treasure's neck swiveled like the chick from the movie, *The Exorcist* and her eyes widened. "I wish the fuck you would!"

"Try me." We both gawked at each other like two raging bulls. "You're a fucking disgrace to the family with that shit you're doing," I told her, just as I always did.

Rocco stood, allowing his displeasure to silence us both. His eyes were piercing as he spoke. It was weird how someone so young carried so much power. "Ms. Newell...I mean Keema. I really do hope you get better," Rocco said to me. "Let's go. Now, Treasure!"

Just like that, Treasure moved toward the door. I rolled my eyes one last time and turned back over towards the wall as everyone left the room. Treasure could fuck with me if she wanted, but I'd become fed up with waiting for her to give me the money she'd promised so many times. Paralyzed or not, manipulation was my key to survival and I was willing to do whatever the fuck it took to get what I wanted.

Chapter 4-
Treasure

"Oh God, Kendrick!" she screamed. "You're killing it, baby!"

That sound of skin against skin sounded over and over again, sometimes fast, sometimes slow; as Kendrick gripped Rasheeda's hips and pounded her from the back.

"You like that dick?" Kendrick asked her, pounding like the pussy had stolen something. He gripped her hips as he repeatedly worked himself in and out of her.

"Yes, baby, I *love* this dick!"

Their sexual escapade meant nothing to me. It didn't even turn me on. It was all about money in my mind. My focus was on trying to get a good shot of Kendrick's face. That would be the key. If I could get his face on video having sex with a sixteen-year-old girl, it was on. There would be absolutely nothing he could say to get out of it.

Usually, Toy worked the flip camera. I always preferred to stay behind the scenes and broker shit, like a real CEO. I usually made the connections with the men, then hooked them up with my girls. I didn't participate in the actual fucking or video-ing; that was for low life bitches, but tonight was different. Since Kendrick was such a big deal, I wanted to be sure nothing went wrong. Toy had never slipped up before, but there was always a first for everything. Besides, there was a reason why she was eighteen and still in the eleventh grade; dumb bitch stayed back two times. That old saying, rang in my head, "If you want something done right, you've got to do it yourself."

I guess that's why I ended up in this closet, too tight for two people. Still, me and Toy were making it work. Shit, we had no choice. Tonight was the biggest night of our operation. Shit was in full effect and there was no room for fuck ups, none at all. The scam we'd been running was my idea. I'd come up with it after watching an episode of 20/20 a year ago and couldn't let it go. I knew it could work if done correctly.

The scam had been thought up by a group of suburban moms in New Jersey. They were running an escort service over Facebook. They'd been running it for two years and had made close to half a million dollars off of it by the time the cops finally caught up to them. When the cops finally snared them, the women weren't the only ones to go down. Dozens of men who were their clients went down, too. Of course they were white; black people knew better than to do some shit out in the open like that.

Myself, Toy, and several other girls had been running that same scam for the past year, but added a little twist to it. All of the clients we were dealing with were grown men, which made sex with us technically statutory rape, especially with the spin we put on it. We'd secretly take pictures and video the men during their sessions with us and collect payment for service…by blackmailing of course. Most of the men were fathers, husbands, entrepreneurs and employees of good companies. The last thing they wanted to do was lose all of that, let alone go to prison. So, although with a little reluctance, they simply paid whatever we requested to make the shit go away.

It had all been going beautifully, but tonight it would get even better. Tonight we were entering the big leagues. We'd snagged a big fish. Shit, as a matter of fact, big wasn't the word for it. *Huge* was more like it. The man we were videoing tonight was Kendrick Morris; one of the most well respected and highly paid pastors in the entire B-More area.

Up until tonight, the men we'd lured in were small fish, most struggling to make ends meet. The most we could get out of them was no more than ten grand, and even that was a stretch. With a mega church in Ellicott City and another location being built in Laurel, MD, Kendrick obviously had plenty of money in his bank account. There was no telling how much we'd be able to get out of him, but we were definitely going to find out.

"Bitch, would you move?" I whispered over my shoulder to Toy who was pressed up against my back. "This closet is too fucking small for all that moving around."

I was already aggravated because I'd received a text an hour ago from one of my homegirls saying that she'd seen Rocco with some bitch. I had no problem with him associating with other women since he'd made it clear from day one that I was his number #1, but there *would* be others. My problem was that she saw him hugged up with the bitch. Now that was a no-no. We had rules; no kissing, no hugging, and no emotional bullshit. Rocco claimed that he only used other women for business and had them suck him off from time to time, which didn't mean anything to him. I would deal with his ass about that later. Right now, I needed to handle business with Rasheeda.

"Toy, get off my back, shit," I whispered a little louder, trying not to let the camera bang against the door and trying to make the least amount of noise as possible. The last thing we needed was for the nigga to hear us.

My arm was sore and my hand was cramping up from standing, trying to hold the camera in one spot for so long. My ankles were also hurting so bad that I had to keep dancing from foot to foot. My damn knees were locking up, too.

"I'm trying to see," Toy said, looking over my shoulder and maneuvering her head back and forth, trying to peer through the narrow gap between the door and the frame.

"For what?"

"I wanna see how big his dick is."

"What?"

"I wanna see how big his dick is," she repeated.

"You tripping."

At that moment, Kendrick slowed his strokes down and looked up towards the closet with a blank stare. Shit, we were caught.

"What's that? I just heard something," he said with caution.

Just when it looked as if he was about to pull out, Rasheeda pulled his hips back towards her and moaned.

"Ohhhh shittt, baby…don't stop. Please don't stop. This dick is too good."

As soon as she was able to get Kendrick to focus again, I breathed a sigh of relief, then shot Toy a 'shut the fuck up look'.

Rasheeda was one of our top money makers. The girl was a stallion, for real, even at sixteen. She was half black and half Samoan with smooth skin, green eyes and a beautiful caramel complexion. Her hair was long, jet black and wavy with a silky shine to it. Along with big breasts, her ass was so fat and well-rounded, even I admired it. The men *loved* her and didn't mind paying the $600 an hour rate.

Suddenly, I felt my phone vibrating. I looked down to see my mother's number on the screen. Even if I weren't hiding in a closet, I wouldn't have answered. I had 99 problems, but she wasn't one. Just like that, Rocco flashed across my mind again. Despite trying to stay focused, that shit still had my blood boiling. I couldn't believe him. Even though I was well aware of how niggas rolled, the shit was still foul.

"Look, look, girl," Toy whispered, grabbing my shoulder. "They're changin' positions. They're changin' positions."

She was right. Kendrick turned Rasheeda towards the closet. We could see his face clearly now.

The sound of his hips against hers started up again, this time even louder. His back shots were hitting her so hard, Rasheeda had to brace herself with her arms just so her ass wouldn't fly off the bed. She then began screaming in pleasure as the headboard banged against the wall and the bedsprings squeaked loudly.

"Damn, girl, he's tearin' her ass up," Toy said. "That dick looks like it's good, too. Who would've ever thought a pastor could put it down like that."

From the sounds coming from Rasheeda's mouth and the look on her face, I had to agree with Toy. I mean, Rasheeda's eyes were damn near cross-eyed and rolling up in her head like she was going to have a seizure. It looked like she was battling with both pleasure and pain at the same time.

My eyes went from Rasheeda's face to Kendrick's. With her eyes lowered and focused, he pounded her ass with deep concentration. Kendrick smirked as well, knowing he was beating her pussy up. I couldn't help noticing how fine the nigga was. His complexion was as brown as honey, and his chiseled chest was cut up more than the average athlete. You could tell that nigga stayed in the gym. Not to mention, he had tons of swag for someone in his late forties.

For a moment his back shots hypnotized me. For a moment I imagined it was me he was fucking. I know I could've given him more for his money than Rasheeda. Instead of an arch in her back, she had a hump like she was scared to truly take the dick. It was obvious she was trying to run from it, but his grip on her hips wouldn't allow her to. My ass was nowhere near as fat as hers, but I would've been throwing it back against every single shot he inflicted. I hated a bitch who couldn't take good dick. Amateurs.

Several moments later, Kendrick finally came. He collapsed onto Rasheeda's back and then onto the bed exhausted. It was understandable. He'd been wearing Rasheeda out for over an hour non-stop. For a while, both just laid in each other's arms until he finally got up, took off his rubber and tossed it into the trash. Kendrick then put his clothes on and paid Rasheeda in cash. Seconds later, he was gone.

Toy was the first out of the closet, damn near knocking me onto the floor. "Damn, Rasheeda, was the dick as good as it looked?"

"It was better," Rasheeda said, wrapping a sheet around her body. She sat up on the bed.

"Girl, it looked like he was killin' you," Toy commented.

"The nigga's dick was all up in my chest. He was a beast!" Rasheeda responded.

Both girls started laughing.

"Fuck all that," I said, ready to get on with business. "Where's the cash?"

As Rasheeda reached for the money, my cell phone vibrated. It was my mother once again. I sent her to voicemail as the money was handed to me. After finally taking my phone off vibrate, I immediately began to count. Blindingly, hundred dollar bill after hundred dollar bill sifted beneath the thumb of my right hand and came to rest snugly in the palm of my left hand. Each bill was crispy and clean, it was also giving off that smell that only real money getters could recognize; that new money smell. I counted out twelve hundred dollars and gave Rasheeda three-hundred. Toy and I was supposed to split the other nine. Instead, I told her she was only getting two-fifty."

"What the fuck is this?" Toy asked in fury.

"You've been demoted! Plus, you were too fucking noisy in the closet. We'll discuss that later, though. Not in front of the hired help," I told her firmly. She knew better than to try me in front of Rasheeda.

"So, how much you think we can get him for?" Rasheeda asked, taking the conversation in a different direction.

She damn near had dollar signs dancing around in her eyes.

I turned to look at Toy who had her arms folded across her chest. She had no input, so I checked her quick.

"Toy, get over it. You still my girl and we gon' get paid together, trust me. Besides, you know this bullshit money right here is not how we really get paid. The big bucks come when the blackmailing starts."

No response. She still fed me attitude.

"He left his rubber in the trashcan. You think we can do something with it?" Rasheeda questioned.

"We probably could. Grab it, bag it and keep it, just in case."

"Okay, but how are we going to get him? Should we say he raped me?" Rasheeda continued.

"Nah," I uttered. "That wouldn't work. The video won't make anyone believe you were being raped at all."

"Sure as hell won't," Toy agreed.

"Well, how about I lie and say I'm pregnant."

I thought about that for a moment. That was a good idea. If it worked, instead of just receiving *one* blackmail payment from him, we could get money from him for the next eighteen years in child support. Damn, Rasheeda had game. If Toy got too far out of pocket, I'd replace her ass with Rasheeda on the administrative side.

"I'll definitely keep that in mind," I told her.

Suddenly, my cell phone rang again. Recognizing Rocco's ringtone, I quickly answered, spazzing on him immediately. "Nigga, where the fuck are you? I heard some shit 'bout you! So, you somewhere with a bitch?"

"Treasure, there's no time for that right now," he said in a low tone, almost like he was whispering.

"What the fuck do you mean ain't no time for that? I wanna …"

"Treasure!" he shouted but still in a loud whisper, inter- rupting me. "I'm in trouble."

Rocco never sounded worried.

Ever.

He was a mandingo type nigga, never fearful, never afraid. Yet, I recognized the distress in his voice.

"What do you mean trouble? What's wrong?"

He groaned in pain.

Pressing my ear tighter to the phone, I said, "Baby, what's wrong?" Now, I was worried.

Rasheeda and Toy were looking at me intently.

He groaned again. "Treasure, there's blood everywhere."

"What? Where are you?"

"Treasure…"

"Rocco, where you at? I'm on my…"

CRACK!!!

The roar of a gunshot filled the phone so loudly that both Rasheeda and Toy heard it.

"Oh my God! Treasure, was that a gunshot?" Toy asked.

"Rocco!" I screamed.

Rocco didn't respond.

"Rocco, answer me!"

The line went dead.

Chapter 5-
Treasure

People and the bright lights of storefronts and traffic lamps darted by my window over and over again as my foot remained pressed firmly on the gas pedal. The rubber of all four tires whined and screeched as I impatiently swerved in and out of the night's traffic. My heart pounded and my adrenaline flooded through my veins like a rampaging river. With one hand on the steering wheel, I managed to repeatedly glance down at my phone and back through the windshield as I dialed number after number with trembling fingers and placed it to my ear. After three rings, Ace, Rocco's best friend answered.

"You heard from him yet?" I asked immediately.

I'd already called him three times in just a short amount of time. It had become like a habit. I had no idea exactly what else to do.

"Nah, I've been callin' around since the last time you called. No one's heard anything from him. No one's even seen him."

"Damn it!" I yelled into the phone. "Where the fuck is he?"

"I'm gonna keep callin' around, Treasure. Somebody has to know something. This definitely ain't like him. Around this time, he would've checked in with someone."

"If you find out anything, please call me, Ace. I don't care what it is. Call me!"

"I got you."

I hung up.

Worry couldn't explain the way I felt. It wasn't even close. It was something much more extreme, while combined with fear. Worry was an understatement. That gunshot I'd heard earlier terrified me even though I'd been raised by gunfire. All I could think was that my baby was dead or lying somewhere bleeding to death. My mind kept playing the possibilities through my head over and over like a video. The shit was torture. It was so bad I even found myself trying to hold back tears.

"There's blood everywhere!" Rocco's words constantly replayed in my mind and stuck with me. Whose blood was he talking about? Was it his? Was it someone else's? What had exactly happened? Who let off that gunshot? So many questions ran through my head in dire need of answers.

Once again, I frantically pressed the recents button on my iPhone and hit Rocco's name. Hoping desperately to hear Rocco's voice, I tightly pressed the phone to my ear as it began to ring.

"Answer, baby," I whispered, while looking around at each person I rapidly passed by, hoping to possibly see him.

One ring turned into two.

The second ring became a third.

"Answer, baby, answer."

After several rings, my call went to voicemail for the twentieth time. That was how many times I'd called him since hearing his troubled voice over an hour ago.

"Fuck!" I screamed into the phone as his voicemail told me he wasn't available and instructed me on how to leave a message. When the beep came, I said, "Rocco, where are you, damn it? Where the fuck are you? You've got me scared to death. Answer the phone, baby, please!"

It felt like I was about to have a heart attack. But as soon as I pressed the end button, surprisingly, my phone began to ring.

"Rocco?" I asked, answering it immediately, hoping it was him.

"Nah, this Ace."

"Have you heard anything?"

"I don't know if it means anything, but maybe you should check out the detail shop he took your car to this mornin'. They may have heard somethin' in a phone conversation while he was there. They may have seen somethin' or someone who can lead us to him. It's worth a try."

That was a good idea. I hadn't thought about it. "Alright, I'm on my way now."

"Keep me posted," Ace said, hanging up.

The detail shop wasn't too far from my current location. He'd taken my car there this morning to get the windows tinted and left me with his 650 BMW, which I whipped wildly through the streets. The shop was owned by a friend of his and located in an industrial area not far from one of Rocco's many stash spots. Everyone knew him in the area so for the past thirty minutes, I'd been stopping by all his hang out spots and questioning all his friends. No one knew anything. If they did, they weren't saying anything. The tires of the Beamer squealed loudly as I reached an upcoming corner and made a hard right onto a side street, jetting in the direction of the detail shop.

My phone rang once again.

"Yeah," I said, placing it to my ear; knowing by the ringtone that it was my mother.

"They're gonna discharge me in the morning. You coming to get me, right?" she asked.

"Ma, I can't talk about that right now."

My eyes were still peeled on every house and person I passed.

"What do you mean you can't talk about it right now?"

"Ma, something happened to Rocco. I really think he's hurt, maybe even worse. He called earlier and…"

"Treasure, damn it, I'm tired of you putting Rocco before me!"

"What are you talking about?"

"You know what the fuck I'm talking about! Everything is always Rocco. Rocco this and Rocco that! I'm your mother. Fuck Rocco!"

"Now is not the time for this shit, Ma!"

"Never disrespect your family over a nigga, Treasure. Remember that, 'cause that same nigga will bring another bitch to your funeral if something happens to you."

"You're tripping right now."

"*I'm* tripping? So, I call to tell you that the hospital is gonna discharge me tomorrow, but *I'm* the one who's tripping?" she spat. "Wow…unbelievable. I'm the one in the fucking wheelchair, Treasure. Do you even care?"

At that moment, I couldn't hold back.

"Yeah, you're in a wheelchair, Ma! I know that! The whole world knows it! You remind us all every damn second of the day!"

My mother attempted to talk, but I wouldn't let her get a word in.

"The reason you're in that wheelchair is because of what you're doing right now; always thinking about yourself! You put yourself in that wheelchair. You were the one who wanted to be grimy and fuck people over, remember? You were the one who couldn't keep it one hundred with people, remember?" I paused then hit her with my final words. "Look, I've gotta find Rocco!"

I jabbed my thumb against the end button, ending the call and tossed the phone onto the passenger seat. A few seconds later, I approached the detail shop. I grabbed the phone and tried Rocco again.

Still, no answer.

After pulling to the curb, I hopped out of the car and stepped out in front of the shop. All the lights were out as I peeped in a dusty window. I couldn't see anything. After glancing around the surrounding area, I climbed back into the car, backed up and pulled into the narrow alleyway beside the shop where they worked on cars. A few moments later, what I saw sent chills down my spine…

My Benz.

Quickly slamming on the breaks, I let my window down to get a closer look at my car. It was parked alone, no other cars in sight. Looking around the area, there was no one else in sight either. Everything was dark and silent, giving me the creeps.

Leaving the BMW running, I jumped out and closed the door. Once again, I looked around and saw no one. When my eyes found their way back to my car, seeing it there gave me an eerie feeling. A strange feeling developed in my gut.

The windows had been tinted just like Rocco had promised. Seeing that made me feel even more uneasy. I couldn't help but wonder if he might possibly be inside. I promptly made my way toward the car. A dog could be heard barking off in the distance. A police siren could also be heard blaring from an even further distance. Even at night, the hood never slept.

The alleyway was so dark. Its only illumination was the beams of the full moon overhead. The closer I walked toward my car, the more nervous I became. Remembering the gunshot, I wondered if the shooting had happened here. If so, was the shooter somewhere near? All the wondering made me approach my car with caution. When I finally reached it, I tried to open the driver's door, but it was locked. I then pressed my face against the window and looked though the dark tint. There was no one inside. The realization relieved me for a moment, but immediately I reminded myself Rocco was still missing.

"Damn," I said with frustration.

Suddenly, an arm wrapped around my neck and viciously snatched me back until I was flat against someone's
chest.

"Ah…" a scream attempted to escape my mouth.

"Shut the fuck up," a voice whispered angrily as the grip
of his forearm tightened, cutting off my windpipe and quieting
my scream before anyone could hear it.

The stranger pressed the tip of a gun directly to my temple. The feel of it horrified me. All I could think about was the
trigger getting squeezed and my head exploding like a pump-
kin.

Pressing his lips to my ear, the stranger whispered, "I
told you I was comin' back for you."

Even in a whisper, I finally recognized the voice. Karma
had finally gotten me. It was Vegas. I wanted to plead, but
couldn't. His forearm was like a boa constrictor. It wouldn't
allow me to speak a word or make a sound. Barely able to
breathe, I grabbed his arm and tried my hardest to release his
grip, but couldn't. Fighting even harder, I still found no luck.

It was obvious I was facing my very last moments on
earth. He'd promised me death for what I'd done to him. Just
like the others, once he got caught in the web of our scam, he
was furious and had made threats, but I didn't take it seriously;
not even the night he'd called during my party. I never expected
to get caught slipping. I never expected him to find me.

"You destroyed my life, you ratchet ass bitch," he said.
"Do you know that?"

Obviously, I couldn't answer. All I could do was make
gasping sounds, trying to get air. Tears began to fall from my
eyes, roll down my cheeks and fall to the ground.

"My wife put me out of my own damn house and now I
can't even see my son because of those fuckin' pictures!"

His grip tightened. It was now so tight I thought my
neck was going to snap like a branch. My ears were dreading

hearing the bones inside it crack.

"You destroyed my life, bitch! My family was my damn world! And your tramp ass took it all away from me!"

If I could just talk, maybe I could weasel my way out of this shit. I wanted to say something to him badly. Maybe, I could cut some sort of deal with him. Maybe I could even beg for my life. I wanted to say anything I could, but his grip wouldn't allow me to.

"But payback is a muthafucka, though. Just like you took my loved ones away from me, I took yours away from you."

What was he talking about?

With pleasure in his voice, he said, "Yeah, I killed that little boyfriend of yours."

My eyes widened at the news.

"Of all the luck, while lookin' for you, I was able to catch him. Yeah, you should've seen it. I blew his head all the way off his shoulders," Vegas bragged.

Hearing the news devastated me. I began to fight harder to break free, but my attempt only made him laugh.

"Yeah," he said, refusing to let up. "I killed him. Now, I'm gonna kill you then head to your house for your mother, too."

Whimpers left my mouth.

Tears fell harder.

"But not before I take that sneaky connivin' pussy of yours," he told me harshly.

With that said, Vegas released me only to turn my body around and slap me across the face with the butt of his gun. The force was so severe it immediately knocked me to the ground and clouded my vision. I could see two of everything. Not wanting to die, I opened my mouth to scream. But before a sound could come out, he shoved the barrel inside.

"Scream and you'll die right here, right now."

There was nothing I could do.

Vegas snatched me to my feet. My knees were wobbly and my head ached as he dragged me over to my car. Once we reached it, he placed the gun to the back of my head, and forced me over the hood. Immediately afterward, he grabbed my leggings and began to force them down to my thighs.

"I'm going to enjoy this," he bragged with delight.

Vegas wiggled his own pants down with his free hand. His dick was stiff already in anticipation. A second later, he viciously forced himself inside of me. Since I was dry, the inside of my pussy felt like it was ripping apart. The pain made me attempt another scream.

"Shut the fuck up before I blow your head off!" he demanded.

I had no choice but to do what he said. My attempt at a scream turned into repeated whimpers as he forced himself into me hard and without mercy. I could only cry as he forcefully drove his dick deeper inside until my pussy felt like it was on fire. Tears began to well up in my eyes and made their way down my cheeks. He'd entered me raw, which was a complete violation. As the tears fell, I couldn't help but wonder if I were crying more over the pain of being raped or the fact of knowing I was going to die as soon as it was over.

Chapter 6-

Keema

"That bitch, Treasure, was *really* serious," I muttered under my breath in disbelief. "She really didn't come to get me."

"Excuse me?" the nurse asked as she wheeled me down the hallway of the hospital towards the lobby. "Did you say something, Ms. Newell?"

"I wasn't talking to you," I snapped. "Just do your job and wheel me out to the front. If I'm talking to you, I'll say your damn name."

"Ms. Newell, there's no need to be disrespectful. That's not necessary."

"Whatever, just do your job and keep pushing." I hated that she had to push me anyway. I could do it my damn self, but she kept saying it was hospital policy. It was bad enough that I had to take the hospital's raggedy ass wheelchair home since Treasure never showed up with mine. The nurse shook her head, but kept rolling me toward the door.

I was furious at Treasure. She'd spoken to me on the phone like I was a stranger, like I wasn't her mother, like it wasn't my pussy she'd popped out of. Who the fuck did she think she was? Who the fuck did she think she was talking to? My blood boiled intensely at the thought. I felt so disrespected, so unappreciated. If I hadn't been in this wheelchair, she wouldn't have tried that. She wouldn't have disrespected me.

I'd called her at least fifteen times since yesterday, and the heifer never answered…not even once. I'd texted and left several messages on her voicemail, but got no response. The bitch had basically left me stranded. The fact that she'd chosen that nigga over me was totally unacceptable. She'd even dropped the ball on Shane. Luckily, I'd gotten our neighbor to go and check on him and to make sure he had food since I'd been gone. Treasure knew better than that. I couldn't wait to talk to that selfish bitch.

As the nurse approached the lobby, I called Ms. Kyle for the umpteenth time. I'd been calling her all morning to see if she knew someone who could come pick me up, but got no response from her either. That was strange, though because Ms. Kyle always answered my calls. If she couldn't, she always got back at me within a short time. Something must've been wrong, but I figured I'd try one last time. Quickly, I went to my contacts list and hit her name.

Once again, Ms. Kyle wasn't answering her phone. Hanging up, the glass doors parted in front of me as I was pushed out into the beautiful fall day. Waiting at the curb was a wheelchair accessible taxi van. All I could do was shake my head. The fact that I had to ride in this shit was so embarrassing, and I hated that it was my only option. Once the hospital staff realized I didn't have a ride home, they immediately called the taxi service. I had an attitude instantly.

The driver, who was African, got out and began to assist me inside. My wheelchair sounded like clunks of metal clashing together as it was loaded onto the van's ramp.

"Be careful, nigga!" I shouted. "I ain't a piece of old furniture. Take it easy."

"Sorry, ma'am," he said with a heavy African accent.

"Fuck being sorry. Be *careful!*"

"Take care, Ms. Newell," the nurse said as she smiled and waved her hand back and forth.

Unfortunately, I didn't return the gesture. Instead, I rolled my eyes and looked the other way. Didn't she know I didn't have shit to smile about? After the driver loaded me safely inside, he closed the door and made his way around to the driver's seat.

"I need you to make a stop before you take me home," I told him, flashing a fifty dollar bill in the air.

"Ma'am, I can't. I have a fare waiting. I was instructed to pick you up and take you directly to your destination so I can make the other fare."

I looked at him like he was crazy. "Look here, Kunta Kinte, Erykah Badu, Shaka Zulu, Roots reject, or whatever your name is. I don't know how things are done in *your* country, but in America it's first come, first serve. I was the first muthafucka in this cab. So, until I decide to get out, I own you."

"Ma'am, first of all, my name is Edabu," he said, pointing to his badge hanging from his rearview mirror. "Secondly, my orders came straight from my dispatcher. I have to do what he says."

"E-doo doo…"

"It's Edabu."

"Well, whatever your name is, I don't give a fuck if you got orders from Barack Obama, I'm not getting out of this cab until you take me exactly where I want to go."

With those words said, I tossed the fifty dollars over the seat to him, folded my arms across my breasts and looked at him straight forwardly like, 'Well, what you gon' do?"

He sighed, but eventually put the van in drive. I gave him the address and displayed a slight smile as we headed there. Within a few minutes, we were on Edmondson Avenue in West Baltimore. Young dope boys in saggy jeans, Jordans, and long white tees were posted on every other corner. Strung out crackheads and prostitutes strolled the strip like mindless zombies.

"This street coming up," I told him.

He slowed, pulled into the right lane, and turned down the side street.

As I watched run down house after run down house pass by my window, I couldn't help but feel anticipation for going to see Mr. Evans. He was an old timer in my old hood, but well respected. He always had the latest info on everything in the hood. Also, whatever you needed, he could get. It didn't matter if it was guns, credit cards, or social security numbers. For what I was planning, a person of his talents was definitely needed.

Last night was the final straw. I'd taken all I was going to take. People were going to pay, no matter who it was. I was going to walk again and I was going to get back at the niggas who'd put me in this chair. But I couldn't do it without Mr. Evans. Even though I knew making a deal with him was like making a deal with the devil; at this point, I no longer cared.

"Right here," I told the driver as we pulled up in front of a convenience store.

The store was owned by Mr. Evans. Nearly everything illegal under the sun went on underneath the roof of the store. You could cash checks without ID, play the Lottery; both legal and illegal, and get passports made. Around back you could even by weed and guns.

Crackheads were posted in front of the store as the driver got out of the van, activated the electronic ramp and assisted me out. I recognized two of them. They'd been around the hood since forever and were most likely never going to leave. Guess they realized they weren't shit a long time ago and had come to accept it. Each of them stared at me, recognizing me instantly. They began to whisper among themselves while they pointed and whispered like I was a side show freak. The shit was absolutely humiliating. It felt like I was on display.

"What the fuck y'all looking at?" I lashed out at them. "Y'all ain't never seen a bitch in a wheelchair before?"

No one answered. They just kept staring.

"I'll be back out in a minute," I told the driver and rolled myself towards the store.

However, before I could even make it all the way inside, I saw that African muthafucka quickly close the back door after the ramp was inside, jump into the driver's side and speed away. I was in complete disbelief. I also knew that this never would've happened to the old Keema. Once again, I was completely humiliated.

As soon as I got inside, the smell of mildew and moth balls invaded my nostrils. The store had been standing for at least fifty years. Leaks in the roof had been patched and re-patched dozens of times. The windows had been busted and the pipes had backed up more times than anyone could count. Basically, the store had definitely earned the stripes of old age.

"Keema, is that you?" Naomi asked from behind the counter.

Damn, I hated being recognized. Naomi and I had gone to high school together. She was a straight hood rat with five kids, the last time I counted. Of course she was a regular down at Social Services. Just before I got locked up we happened to be down there at the same damn time for an appointment. She was milking the system, of course.

"What's good, girl?" I asked, forcing a smile. Obviously, I didn't want to speak but had to.

"Wowwww," she said, hugging me. "Girl, I ain't seen you in years. Where you been?"

"Just trying to stay out the way. You know how it is?"

Her eyes looked down at the wheelchair sympathetically. "Girl, I heard about what happened. I'm so sorry for you. Why they do that to you?"

Knowing her ass was just snooping for information so she could gossip to the neighborhood I said, "Is Mr. Evans here?"

"Yeah, what you need him for?"

Damn, she was nosey. "It's personal. Is he back there?"

"Yeah, hold on," Naomi responded. She grabbed the phone and made a call to the back room. Moments later, she told me, "Go ahead, girl. You need any help?"

"Nah, I'm good."

"You need any food stamps? I'm selling 'em for one-third the price."

"Nah, I'm good," I said fast as I could. The bitch was still fishing for info. She just wanted to see if I was still on the system.

I rolled down an aisle that led to the back room. As I approached the door, a tall, stocky man with a bald head and big ears appeared. Undoubtedly, he was Mr. Evans' henchman.

"Hold up," he said when I reached the door.

I stopped.

He began to frisk me, carefully looking for a gun or weapon of any kind.

"I'm clean, damn," I told him, hating having his heavily calloused hands all on me.

When he was finished, he stepped to the side and allowed me in. Mr. Evans was sitting behind a huge, junky desk; papers filled to the top. He was tall, grey haired and his complexion was that of rusty brown water. By now, my guess was that he was in his late-sixties. His eyes had a sneaky sort of look to them, along with a mischievous smirk, which exposed his yellowish, discolored teeth from years of smoking. He always looked like he was up to something. He looked at me skeptically for several seconds.

"Hey, Mr. Evans, do you remember me? My name is Keema," I said.

Keeping a doubtful look on his face, he eyed me up and down suspiciously. "Yeah, I remember you, Keema. I heard you was dead."

"Nah, I'm not dead."

"So I see. What business you got with me?"

"Actually, I need a favor."

"A favor, huh?" he asked, glancing at his henchman and then leaning back into his chair.

"Yeah, I…"

My cell phone rang.

Quickly, snatching it from my purse, I glanced at Ms. Kyle's number. "Sorry, Mr. Evans, I gotta take this."

He nodded, but kept his eyes on me as if he didn't trust me.

Answering the phone, I said, "Ms. Kyle, this isn't a good time. I've gotta call you back."

She ignored my haste. "Are you okay, Keema? I didn't have my phone with me earlier. When I got it, I noticed all your calls."

"I'm alright, but I…"

"I just called the hospital and they told me you were discharged."

"Yes, I am but…"

"Well, thank God you're okay. Dinero and I were worried sick. I hate that you didn't want us to come visit while you were there, so he's gonna be so happy to know that you're going home. Here he is."

Mr. Evans still looked at me like I was a puzzle he was trying to figure out. It was annoying, but I realized in his business, it was hard to trust people. Snakes were everywhere.

"Hey, Ma," Deniro's voice came through the phone. He sounded so excited.

"Hey, baby."

"Where you at?"

"Handling something important."

"Ms. Kyle said you were going home today."

"I am. I just got to handle something first."

"Guess what, I got an A on my math test, so Ms. Kyle

gave me five dollars."

"Aww, that's so good, baby."

Mr. Evans sighed loudly, signaling me that his time was valuable.

"Deniro, I gotta go. I'll call you back later, okay?"

"When am I gonna see you? I miss you," he whined.

"Soon Deniro…real soon. Now, I gotta go."

"Alright, I love you, Ma."

"I love you, too."

The two of us hung up.

"I'm sorry about that, Mr. Evans."

"Keema, I'm a busy man. What is it that you need?"

"Mr. Evans, I need someone robbed."

His eyebrows rose slightly. Both he and his henchman, glanced at each other then back at me.

"Robbed? That's a tall order; big boy shit."

"I know."

"Why do you need this person robbed?"

"It's personal, but I swear it'll be worth your while."

"How worth it?"

"*Really* worth it."

"And what are you willing to pay?" Mr. Evans questioned.

"I don't have any money, but I can guarantee you this isn't a lick you want to pass up. You can keep thirty percent of the money."

Obviously interested, Mr. Evans leaned forward and placed his ashy forearms on the surface of the desk, giving me all his attention. "I'm listening," he said.

"They getting real money, Mr. Evans. I mean, at least a hundred thousand is free for the taking at all times."

The two men shared glances again.

"And as I said, you can keep thirty percent."

"Fifty," Mr. Evans said stone faced.

"But…"

"It's my men, my guns, my sacrifices. Fifty percent is non-negotiable."

"Alright," I finally complied. I hadn't done this in a while and felt beyond rusty.

"That's not all."

I looked at him closely.

"I need you to hear me and hear me good. This better not be no bullshit. There had better be not a penny less than one hundred thousand dollars in this shit for grabs. A penny less, and your life will be expected payment," Mr. Evans explained.

His eyes were staring deeply into mine with absolutely no nonsense in them. They didn't even blink. His expression was stone and serious, letting me know that this was not a game. My ass was definitely on the line if this didn't work out.

I'd heard rumors about people getting their bones broken, and their faces caved in for trying to go back on deals they made with Mr. Evans. I'd heard stories of young goons getting their skulls caved in with wrenches and crow bars. I'd even heard of niggas getting kidnapped and stuffed in the back of cars. He wasn't a joke. He played for keeps. A lump developed in my throat and my heart rate sped up, knowing I was truly making a deal with the devil.

"Once you agree, there's no turning back. Do you understand me?" he asked.

I nodded. "Yeah, I got you."

"Your word is just as good as a signed contract," he said obviously satisfied.

Nervously, I exhaled a deep breath unaware I was holding it. The old man had me shook.

"Alright, now who's the guy you want us to rob?"

Both men were watching me directly, expecting my answer.

With a smirk, I said, "Oh, it's not a guy at all."

"Then who is it?"

"It's my daughter."

Chapter 7-
Treasure

My body wouldn't stop shaking. My hands wouldn't stay steady. My stomach wouldn't stop feeling queasy. My anger wouldn't subside. The tears wouldn't stop falling. The ramifications of being violated felt like a flesh eating disease. Damn, I needed some weed to calm me down.

"You should call the cops on his nasty ass," Toy urged me. "You should call them right now."

"I can't," I told her as I exhaled chronic smoke for the hundredth time since last night. "You know I ain't no mutha-fucking snitch."

She looked at me like I was crazy. "Treasure, it ain't about snitchin'. That nigga *raped* you. He violated you. He should be in jail right now. He should be in a cell with some big nigga named Bubba stuffin' a long dick up in his ass so he can see just how the shit feels. I mean, damn, girl, look at that big ass bruise on your face. Don't you want to see him punished?"

"Hell yeah, I want to see him punished, but it's going to be done *my* way. Trust and believe, I'm going to get mine. I put that on everything I love. The nigga is going to get dealt with to the tenth power. Simply going to jail ain't enough. I want more."

I could still smell Vegas' cheap ass drug store cologne. I could still smell the years of cigarette smoke seeping from his pores. I could still smell the liquor on his breath. My ears could still hear his grunts and moans as he forcefully pressed inside of me. I could still hear him calling me bitches and hoes with every thrust. The shit was sickening.

"Well, how are you gonna do it?" Toy asked.

"I'm not sure, but when I'm done he's gonna wish he was never born. He's gonna wish he'd never met me or even heard my damn name."

Toy gazed at me.

"He's gonna wish he never fucked with me. *And* I'm going to get the money he owes me. The perverted muthafucka thinks he ain't got to pay up. He thinks this changes things. He thinks I'm too scared to go through with the extortion. But he's wrong. I'm going hard on his ass, even harder than before."

I had a whole bunch of things planned for his ass. I just didn't quite know which one to carry out first.

"I can't believe that muthafucka did this to me!" I yelled out. "If that car hadn't pulled up last night, making him turn around and giving me enough time to run, he would've killed me."

Toy shook her head, rolled her eyes and got up from the bed. She muttered something about karma.

"What?" I asked.

She turned to me, then placed her hands on her hips. "Look, Treasure, I don't mean to sound heartless, but this is the game you chose to play."

"So, what the fuck are you saying? That I deserved what happened?"

"I ain't sayin' you deserved it, but I am sayin' you need to be more loyal to those who are loyal to you."

My eyebrows crinkled. I knew what this was about. Toy

still felt some kind of way about me keeping a bigger share of the money from Kendrick. And if she did, shit wasn't going to change. The scam had been my idea from the jump. It was me who lured in the victims. It was me who brokered the deals. I deserved the bigger profits. *Fuck them bitches*, I thought. *All they do is lie on their backs and take dick.*

"So, you're still tripping about that damn money?" I questioned.

"Hell yeah, Treasure. We're supposed to be partners. We're supposed to be friends."

"Ain't no damn room for friendship when it comes to money. You know that, Toy. Besides, who told you we were partners. This is *my* operation. You work for me."

Her eyes narrowed at me. "That's fucked up, Treasure."

"I can't believe you," I told her. "I was raped, my boyfriend is dead and you're sitting here thinking about a petty few dollars."

Hearing myself mention Rocco's murder shifted something inside of me. My heart broke. I bit my bottom lip, dropped my head and closed my eyes. The tears began to fall for the third time today.

Even after hearing Vegas say he'd killed Rocco last night, a part of me just didn't want to accept it. I couldn't let go of my denial. Several times I called Rocco's phone, hoping I'd hear his voice, hoping against all odds he'd survived somehow. Each time, though, I continued to get no answer, only his voicemail.

Toy looked at me with the least bit of compassion. Then, I could've sworn I saw that bitch display some type of smirk as I wiped away tears. Feeling an urge to try again, I picked up my phone, hit Rocco's name and waited for the call to connect. Disappointment invaded my spirit once again when the call went directly to voicemail. This time, the phone didn't even ring.

"I can't believe he's gone," I said between sobs.

"So, do you believe Vegas? Do you believe he really

killed Rocco?"

I shook my head before nodding it. "Yes, I do," I stated in a low tone.

"Well, if he is, you need to get over it," Toy mumbled.

"Damn, how did I let a man get me shook up like this? I was never supposed to fall in love. It was always supposed to be M.O.D; Money Over Dick."

Toy let out a slight chuckle, getting over her little mean-ingless beef with me. "Yeah," she agreed. "I'm still surprised myself. I've never seen you so gone over a dude before. Shit, y'all were only fuckin' around for what…about eight months."

"Yeah, but I guess it was because he wasn't just a dude, Toy. He was different from the others. He was special."

Toy glanced at her watch. "Oh snap, Treasure, we're late!" She stood up.

"Late for what?" I asked, looking up at her with blurred vision. The tears were clouding my eyesight.

"Church."

Damn, she was right. But obviously, after what I was going through now, our scam was the last thing on my mind.

"I can't, Toy. Go without me."

"What do you mean?"

"I'm not up for it today. Ain't it obvious?" I asked laying my head back against the sofa.

"Uh-uh, Treasure, we got money to make. You know today is important. Get your ass up," Toy responded. "We've gotta do this. Look, I know you're hurtin', but we can't let that slow shit down. We'll lose too much if we don't get to that church right now and get this business handled."

Toy ran to her room, before coming back with an outfit in her hand. "Hurry up," she said, tossing me the leopard print leggings and a black v-neck t-shirt.

"Toy, look you…"

She quickly cut me off. "Treasure, I don't wanna hear shit else about Rocco. You can mourn later. Right now we need to get this money. And don't forget to call Rasheeda back. She called here lookin' for you. She said it's an emergency."

"Yeah, yeah," I replied reluctantly while getting dressed.

Moments later, we were in Toy's car headed to the church. While driving, I couldn't help but wonder if my car was okay after purposely having to leave it at the detail shop. I also wondered if Vegas' crazy ass was stalking my shit hoping I would show up so he could go for round two. Damn, I had to figure out the safest way to get it without running into him.

Suddenly, my thoughts were distracted when my phone rang. I can admit, that I don't pray as often as I should, but this time I closed my eyes and silently asked God to somehow let it be Rocco. With him being dead, it was a crazy request, but who didn't believe in miracles every once in a while?

Opening my eyes, I looked down at my phone and got an instant attitude after seeing my mother's name. From the amount of times she'd called, I'm sure she was worried sick about me, but I still didn't feel like dealing with that shit right now. I was on a mission to get my money and some much needed revenge. Everything else would have to wait.

∾

It was about 12:30 in the afternoon as we pulled into the church's parking lot. The sprawling church was about two stories high and looked more like a cathedral with its gables, huge stained glass windows, plush green lawns, and freshly pressure washed walkways. The parking lot was full, boasting a loyal congregation of thousands. With service obviously over, each of them was now making their way out of the church and across the lot.

"Damn, we're too late," Toy said in frustration.

Getting back in business mode, I told her, "Everything's still good. Just find a parking spot."

As we rode around the crowded lot, we slowly passed Kendrick's reserved parking space. Between its bright yellow lines was a new black XJL Jaguar with thirty-day tags. The price tag on his whip was at least seventy-five thousand, so obviously the church's tithes and offerings were pretty hefty.

After Toy finally found a space and parked, I flipped down my visor and looked closely into the mirror. My eyes were still a bit puffy, but it didn't matter. What I was about to do didn't require me to look cute even though I applied some lip gloss and played with my weave.

"Alright, I'll be back," I said to Toy while climbing out of the car.

"Make that money!" she yelled back.

As several churchgoers gawked at my inappropriate church attire and whispered, I continued to strut across the lot and towards the front of the church with my jiggling ass in tow. They were no doubt passing judgment like they weren't out at the club the night before or fucking out of wedlock. That's what I hated most about church folks. They sat up in church every damn Sunday looking down on the rest of the world like their own shit didn't stink. But what they didn't know was that I didn't give a fuck what they thought. I didn't have plans on listening to a sermon, getting struck with the Holy Ghost, dancing in the aisles or singing with the choir. I was here on business.

As I approached the church's entrance, Kendrick was standing there in a long, beautiful wine colored robe as he shook hands with each exiting person. His back was turned towards me so he had no idea I was approaching.

"Yes, child, we must *run* from sin," I heard him tell a woman as he held her hand in his. "We must not let it dwell in our hearts. Anything that is unholy, we must not partake in it."

Ain't that a bitch!

All I could do was shake my head.

He was taking a sip from his bottled water when I placed my shiny lips to his ear, and whispered, "Does that mean you're not supposed to fuck young teenage girls?"

Instantly recognizing my voice, Kendrick spit a mouthful of water to the ground and turned around. "Oh, Lord, have mercy," he said as soon as his eyes rested on me.

The lady he'd been speaking to stood at his side, trying to be nosey.

"Uh, Ms. Jackson, I will speak to you later," Kendrick said knowing he was in trouble.

She eyed me up and down. "Is everything okay, Pastor?"

I folded my arms over my chest and shifted all my weight to one leg, making my ass and hips stand out even further than before.

"Yes, Ms. Jackson," he said, placing a hand on her back and ushering her off while still trying to keep a fake smile on his face.

As soon as Ms. Jackson was out of listening distance, Kendrick pulled out a handkerchief and began to dab his forehead as he turned back toward me. Swallowing a thick lump in his throat, he said, "Now, what can I do for you young lady?"

"Did you like the other day?"

"The other day?" Kendrick asked as if he had no idea what I was talking about.

There was obvious uneasiness in his smile as he kept glancing from me to each person who passed by, obviously wanting to know who I was and what business I had with their man of God.

"Yes, the other day."

"Uh…uh…uh, I'm not quite sh…sh…sure what you're talking about," he stuttered nervously.

I smiled. "Come on now, Rev. You know what I'm talking about. Didn't you like the way my girl sucked your…"

Before I could finish my sentence, Kendrick screamed, "Lord Jesus Christ!" then bowed his head as he placed his hand on my shoulder like he was praying for me. "Oh merciful Lord, please bless this child!"

People continued to look at us as they passed.

"Just saying a little prayer for this young woman,"

Kendrick said to them as he raised his head. "God loves *all* his children. Yes, he does."

At that point, I couldn't help but laugh, which pissed him off.

He stepped closer to me once the coast was clear. "Bitch, what are you trying to do to me? Why are you here? What do you want?"

"You got a nice little hustle going on here, Rev."

"It's not a hustle. Besides, I go by Pastor Morris not Reverend."

"It *is* a damn hustle if your hypocritical ass is in charge of a damn congregation. You should be ashamed of yourself."

He dabbed his forehead again and whispered to himself, "Dear God, have mercy."

"The collection plate must be nice and fat," I told him. "I mean, look at the size of this place. It's obvious you're getting money. I saw the new Jag in your parking space. Plus, you normally ride around town in a Porsche Cayenne."

Nervously, Kendrick whispered something else to himself about God having mercy and forgiving him.

I looked at him seriously. "Look here, Reverend. You've got a nice hustle going on and I want in."

He dabbed his forehead again. Sweat poured down his face, causing him to loosen his collar.

"You're going to give me thirty thousand dollars by the end of this coming week and another thirty thousand by the end of the month."

"Bitch!" Kendrick responded loudly before he could catch himself. Realizing he'd said it loudly enough to bring attention to himself, he swiftly looked around, smiled and looked back at me. In a much lower voice just above a whisper, he said furiously, "I don't have that kind of money."

"The fuck you don't. That car of yours cost you almost eighty racks. Sell that muthafucka if you need to. I don't care how you get the money. Just get it."

"You're crazy if you think I'm going to give you that amount of money," he said before turning to walk away.

Grabbing Kendrick by his shoulder and turning him around, I reached into my purse and pulled out several photos. "How do you think your congregation will feel when they see these?" I displayed a wicked smile. "These would be a nice little addition to the church announcements wouldn't they?"

Taking the pictures, the color flushed from his face as he saw himself and sixteen-year-old Rasheeda in the middle of the nasty. His mouth dropped. He couldn't speak. His knees looked as if they were going to go weak.

"I've got it on video, too."

"Lord please forgive me," was all he could manage to whisper, as his eyes continued to stare at the photos.

"Look, Reverend, fuck all that Lord forgive me shit. The jig is up. But the question is, how badly do you want to keep this a secret?"

He raised his eyes from the photos and gave me a weak sympathetic look. "Please," he pleaded.

"Fuck that. Get my money by the end of this upcoming week or I'll make sure the video and photos get distributed to everyone in your congregation. I'll even send a special deluxe edition to the police."

"Oh God," Kendrick replied. It looked like he was going to faint.

"When I'm finished with you, God won't even be able to help. Try me if you think it's a game."

"Daddy, daddy!" a little girl in a cream dress screamed as she ran up from out of nowhere.

"Hey, baby," Kendrick said as he bent down and planted a kiss on her cheek. He then slyly stuffed the pictures into his robe.

At that moment, a lady with an ugly, satin mother of the bride looking suit also walked up and kissed him on the cheek. "Hi, honey," she said to him.

Kendrick cleared his throat. "Hello, sweetheart."

"Oh, is this your wife?" I asked excitedly.

Kendrick gave a nervous pleading look as if to say, "Please don't say anything to her. Please don't."

"Yes, I'm the First Lady," she stated with a proud tone.

"Hi, I'm Bria," I lied, extending my hand.

"Nice to meet you, Bria," she said as we shook hands. "I've never seen you here before. Are you a new member of the church? And what happened to your face, dear? Are you okay?"

Kendrick stepped back behind her and began throwing up more waves and hand signals than a first base coach as he silently mouthed to me, "I'll get your money. I swear I will."

His wife turned in time to see him waving. He immediately switched his waves and hand signals to repeated swats, as if he was swatting away something.

"Baby, what's wrong?" she asked.

"Flies, baby. Just swatting away some of these flies."

"Not, I'm not a member but your husband is a big supporter of my business," I said, causing her to face me again.

Kendrick's eyes increased to the size of golf balls.

"Oh, really? Well, what kind of business are you in?"

"Well I'm in the…"

"Good Lord have mercy!" Kendrick shouted as he grabbed his heart and dropped to one knee like he was in pain. The nigga was obviously faking a heart attack.

"Baby, are you okay," his wife asked worriedly as she knelt down beside him. "You don't look good."

"I'm sick, baby," he told her. "I think it was something I ate. I think it was Ms. Jackson's potato salad."

Slyly he glanced up at me.

"One week," I silently mouthed to him before turning around and heading back to the car.

Chapter 8-

Keema

My wheelchair made that electronic whirring sound as I maneuvered it with the tiny joystick at the end of the right armrest. Since I'd been confined to it for so long, obviously I got plenty of practice. These days, I was as fast and talented with it like a fucking race car driver. And since I knew every inch of our rented, one-story handicap accessible house in Woodlawn, I never bumped into anything, not even in the dark.

Drawers were pulled out. Papers, envelopes and mail were strewn about the floor, countertops and tables. The living room was practically a mess as I wildly rambled through anything and everything I could reach, or get my hands on. Anything that was of no use immediately got carelessly tossed to the floor or over my shoulder.

"Damn it!" I yelled, pissed off.

Once again, I rolled back to Treasure's room and stopped at its open door. Her room looked like a tornado had ripped through it without mercy. Actually, instead of a tornado, it had been me. Just like I'd done the rest of the house, I tore her room apart looking for more money. I rambled through her pockets, searched her drawers, shoe boxes, closet, between her mattresses, behind her dresser, and inside her clothes hamper. I was as desperate and relentless as a crack head who'd dropped their very last rock in a dark alleyway.

I searched *everywhere* but still hadn't been able to find more than twelve thousand. All I found were countless receipts for clothes and a bunch of overdue bills. The receipts themselves totaled nearly thirty thousand dollars because she fucked with nothing but Chanel, YSL, Hermes, Prada and every other expensive designer on the racks, no knock offs. The shit pissed me off, especially after everything I'd taught her. It was obvious that dumb bitch was shopping instead of stacking her paper. No wonder she always brushed me off when I talked about my surgery.

As I looked at the mess I'd made, panic began to set in. Mr. Evans' threat of killing me if there wasn't a hundred stacks waiting for him and his goons played itself over and over in my mind. One hundred thousand was a lot of money, and I knew he was serious. Mr. Evans wasn't a game. He didn't play. If he said he'd kill you, you'd better believe he meant it.

"Fuck," I said to myself, beating my closed fists against both sides of my head.

With Treasure getting serious money off of that scam of hers and from Rocco, I thought for sure she'd have more money. If not a hundred thousand, at least something I could work with. Still sitting at her bedroom door, I said desperately, "There has to be a larger stash around here. It just has to be."

I glanced at my watch. Mr. Evans had told me he'd be calling in a few minutes. Since I'd made the deal with him, he'd called several times last night, and started again early this morning; milking me for as much information on Rocco and Treasure as possible. He wanted to know everything about them and how they got money. The last thing he wanted was a surprise. He'd made that absolutely clear to me. If that wasn't enough to think about, the fact that I hadn't spoken to Treasure in two days had me worried.

Even someone from her school called and told me she hadn't been there in over a week. Every time I called her phone, she never picked up. I'd even called Toy, but hadn't gotten a response from her either. I kept telling myself not to panic; that maybe her and Rocco had gone on a last minute trip out of town. But regardless of where Treasure was or what she was doing, I needed her to come home soon. She was the key to a successful plan with Mr. Evans.

I dropped my chin to my chest and closed my eyes, stressed out. I realized that I'd gotten myself in way over my head with the amount I told Mr. Evans he'd be able to get. How could I have been so fucking stupid? What was I thinking? Instead of going off of anger, I should've thought the plan through much more thoroughly.

Hearing my phone go off, I wheeled over towards the coffee table and glanced down at the screen. It was a text message from Lucky telling me to call him.

"Fuck you, Lucky!" I said out loud. There was no way he was going to get a reply. Since his ass wanted to go off and marry some bitch, I had nothing else to say to his ass.

I was just about to grab a cigarette when suddenly there was a knock at the front door. Once again the wheelchair made its whirring sound as I made my way down the hall to the living room and opened the door. Standing there were three young dudes I'd never seen before. Each of them dressed in black jeans, Nike Foamposite sneakers and black hoodies. Their eyes locked on me immediately with scowls on their faces.

"Can I help you?" I snapped.

"Get the fuck out the way," one of them said disrespectfully as he led the other two inside, brushing past me like I wasn't even there.

"Hey," I responded. "This is my damn house! What the fuck do you think you're doing?"

Ignoring me, the three men began to make their way

from room to room.

"Get the fuck out of my house!" I belted.

"Keema, there's no need to be so belligerent and disrespectful towards my associates," Mr. Evans' voice said from behind me.

I turned in my chair to see Mr. Evans standing at my door leaning on a cane. Immediately, my attitude changed. "Oh, Mr. Evans, I didn't know they were with you."

Silently, I wondered how the hell he knew where I lived. I hadn't told him. On top of that, I'd just seen him yesterday. He'd been calling all along. Why would he stop by now instead?

Hearing doors slam throughout the house, I turned to see one of the goons standing at the entrance to the hallway with his arms folded across his chest. I had to admit, even with the long scar that ran down the right side of his face, he was sexy as shit. He stared directly at me with no emotion, all about business.

"Nobody's here," one of the other goons told Mr. Evans as both men came out of my room.

"So, how many people live here?" Mr. Evans questioned.

"Just me, Treasure and my son, Shane."

"Any guns in the house?"

"No."

"Now, don't fuck with me Keema. There better not be any guns in here whatsoever when this shit goes down. Do you understand me?" Mr. Evans asked firmly.

I nodded quickly.

Mr. Evans began to walk around like he owned the place while his goons stood side by side watching me. "What the fuck happened in here? Looks like the place has been robbed already," he said before sitting down on the couch.

"Oh no. My daughter was getting ready to rearrange the furniture so I can move around a little better. Things are just all over the place right now."

For several moments, Mr. Evans said nothing. He just looked me directly in my eyes as if searching for something like he knew I was lying. The shit made me uncomfortable.

"Mr. Evans, I hope you don't think everything was supposed to go down today because we never discussed that. Besides, the money is not even here."

He immediately raised his eyebrows. "So, when is the money gonna be here?"

"Soon."

"How soon?"

"It shouldn't be much longer. It's just that my daughter's boyfriend had to make a quick trip out of town, but he'll be back in a day or two." The lies continued. "So, what's the plan?"

"Don't worry about the plan. I came today just to check things out and to make sure there won't be any surprises."

"But how are you gonna do it?" I pried.

Mr. Evans leaned forward and looked at me even more deeply than before. "You sure ask a lot of questions."

"Yeah," the goon with the scar down his face agreed. "Like a damn cop."

I was tired of Scarface. "Look, I ain't no damn cop. I just wanna know how it's gonna be done. Like, can you guys make it look like a robbery? It has to look like I didn't have anything to do with it. Can you flip me over in my wheelchair or something?"

"For the last time, I don't need any help doing my fucking job. You just tell me when the money is here and I'll do the rest," Mr. Evans boasted.

This time my only response was a head nod.

"This boyfriend better show up soon, and as I said before, there better be nothing less than a hundred thousand in here. Keep your phone on you at all times," Mr. Evans told me. "If I call, and you don't answer, that's your ass."

With those words said, he got up from the couch then headed out of the door with his henchmen not far behind. For a few minutes, I couldn't move. Those minutes soon turned into an hour. I just sat there wondering what the fuck I was gonna do if Rocco didn't drop off that amount of cash. Then a knock came at the door again.

"Shit," I said, thinking Mr. Evans had come back to terrorize me some more.

For a moment, I'd thought about not answering, but realized he'd probably just kick the door in because he knew I was there. Then he'd *really* be pissed. Reluctantly, I wheeled myself across the room and opened the door. I was surprised by who was standing there. It wasn't Mr. Evans or any of his goons.

It was Rocco.

Without a word, Rocco walked past me with his arm in a sling and a black, leather backpack hanging off of his shoulder. He looked like shit. Not only did his shirt have blood on it, but it looked like he hadn't slept in days.

"What the hell happened to you?"

He didn't answer. Instead, he headed straight towards the couch.

"Did you get into a fight? Where's Treasure?"

Still, he said nothing. He simply pulled a gun from his belt, sat it on the table and grimaced in pain as he sat down and leaned back into the cushions. At that moment, I began to think he was obviously there to drop off some money or cook up some heroin like he normally did. I'd actually witnessed him cook up a full kilo numerous times. Realizing that, it dawned on me to call Mr. Evans, hoping that if Rocco didn't have a hundred thousand on him, he could at least lead Mr. Evans and his goons to it. I was getting ready to roll to another room and dial until I remembered Mr. Evans saying he didn't want any surprises. He wanted the money *here*, nowhere else. That meant he probably wouldn't take too kindly to having to do any extra traveling. My life was on the line so I couldn't take any chances.

I rolled over to Rocco. "Are you okay?"

Still leaning back into the cushions with his head raised to the ceiling, he finally said, "I've got problems, Keema. Somebody did some real foul shit to me."

"What did they do? Where's Treasure?" I asked again. Now, I was nervous.

"I don't know. I haven't talked to her. I had to turn my phone off."

"Why?"

"I can't discuss that."

"Well, is my daughter safe at least?"

Rocco nodded his head. "Oh, she should definitely be safe. I'm the one who got into some shit, not her."

"But someone at her school called and said she hasn't been there. I thought she might've been with you."

"Well, that's nothin' to worry about because Treasure never goes to school."

I shook my head in agreement. I didn't even see how the hell she was passing. Knowing Treasure, she was probably fucking the principal. But I still couldn't help but wonder why Treasure wasn't answering my calls, but quickly got distracted when I looked at the knot in Rocco's pockets; no doubt filled with money as usual.

Placing my hand on his lap, I said, "Talk to me, Rocco. What did they do? And who did it?" My eyes dropped to the bulge again, which immediately turned me on. I needed it. I came up with an idea. "Rocco, I know what your problem is," I stated softly.

He looked at me.

I squeezed his thigh. "You need somebody to hold you down, somebody to watch your back."

He watched me intently.

"I know how treacherous these streets are. You can't

make it out here alone. And you definitely can't make it out here with a little girl for a wifey. You need a woman."

My hand rose up his thigh.

"You need someone who's been through what you're going through. If you had that, whatever happened to you wouldn't have happened. A real woman wouldn't have let it go down like that."

He remained silent; just stared at me like I was the one who did something to him. Even though he always gave me that look, I continued.

"Rocco, I've gotta be honest. I've wanted to be yours ever since Treasure introduced me to you. I've envied her ever since. I felt like she was so lucky. But I knew she could never give you what I could. I knew she couldn't handle you. I knew you should've been with me, but I just couldn't say it."

My eyes searched his.

"Rocco, now I'm saying it. I have feelings for you. They won't go away."

My hand rose to his crotch and squeezed.

"Baby, I could be your most loyal soldier, especially if I was out of this chair. If you could get me out of it, I'd be able to show you exactly what a real woman is made of. You'd never have to worry about these streets or this game crossing you again. With me, you would have eyes behind your head."

His dick was now swollen in his jeans.

"Baby, let me be yours, Rocco. Please get me out of this chair so I can be your ride or die bitch."

I quickly unzipped his jeans, pulled his dick from his boxers and lowered my warm mouth down over his thick shaft; surprised that he didn't refuse. He closed his eyes and leaned his head back, releasing a masculine moan as I began to cram as much of him in my mouth and down my throat as possible. From there, I began to hit him with *every* trick I knew, knowing my experience gave my head skills a huge advantage over Treasure's. She hadn't been on the planet long enough to know how to suck a dick as good as me or even *half* as good as me.

"Please, Rocco," I begged in-between gulps and swallows. "Let me be yours, baby."

Viciously I feasted on him, devouring every inch. I was determined to prove to him that *women* sucked the *entire* dick. Only *girls* suck half or just the head. I had to prove the dick didn't intimidate me, no matter how big.

Rocco began to moan my name. With each moan, I went harder, refusing to let up while massaging his huge balls. They began to swell to the size of golf balls. I knew he was going to let off soon and I had every intention of swallowing his babies. He grabbed the back of my neck and began to thrust his hips upwards, needing so badly to release.

"I'm gettin' ready to cum, Keema," he moaned.

I sucked more furiously as he thrusted in and out of my mouth. The both of us were focused on making him cum. My mouth wanted it and his dick needed it.

"Oh shit. Here it comes!" he shouted.

I was anxious to taste it all. But suddenly, just before he gushed, the living room door swung open, causing us to stop and jerk our heads in that direction. Both of our eyes widened at who was standing there.

Chapter 9-

Keema

"Keema, suck Rocco's dick!" Shane said, pointing at me with one hand while covering his mouth with the other. His eyes were wide open in surprise as he stood at the open door jumping up and down while looking directly at us. "Keema, suck Rocco's dick!"

"Shit, Shane!" I yelled, wiping slob from the corners of my mouth, super embarrassed.

"Fuck," Rocco said rapidly jumping up, turning his back and struggling to place himself back into his pants. His dick remained rock hard.

"Keema, suck Rocco's dick!" Shane shouted again, still pointing. He was laughing now.

"Boy, shut your fat ass up!" I yelled at him as I quickly rolled across the room and slammed the door, hoping no one had heard him. "Why the hell are you home so early? Did you get fired?"

Treasure had gotten Shane a job at Home Depot as a parking lot attendant from ten a.m. to six p.m. and it was barely four o'clock. Not sure how she'd managed to pull that off, but his bullshit ass paycheck did come in handy. However, he was always supposed to call before he got on the bus to come home.

"Shane, sick," he said.

"Then go to your room!"

I glanced over at Rocco. He was still attempting to get that monster back into his pants without getting it caught in the zipper while his back was still turned to us. I wasn't done with him yet. I needed that money, and I damn sure wasn't gonna let Shane's slow ass come in-between me and my cash.

I wheeled myself over to Rocco.

"I can't believe I let you do that," he said. "I just can't believe it. This is fucked up."

"Don't worry about it, baby. Shane won't tell anyone. He's you know…" I did mini circles into the air with my index finger. "A little special."

"That's not the point."

"Ewww Keema nasty," Shane blurted out.

At that moment, I wheeled myself around and gave Shane an evil look. "Go to your damn room, Shane…now!" I demanded. He couldn't stop smiling, but quickly followed my orders.

"Rocco, don't worry about that. Trust me, I'll make sure he doesn't repeat what he saw."

I grabbed Rocco's hand and tried to usher him to the bedroom to finish the job. I was desperate and should've been ashamed of myself, but I wasn't thinking straight at all. I needed to walk again and I needed to get Mr. Evans off my ass. Nothing else mattered. I knew if I could get him back into my mouth, I'd be able to get him do what I wanted.

"Chill out, Keema," he demanded.

"Just let me talk to you back here in the bedroom," I pleaded with him, the desperation in my voice evident. "Come on."

Snatching away from me, Rocco shouted, "I said chill

out with that shit!"

I finally stopped and sat there in silence.

"What happened shouldn't have happened," he told me. "That shit was foul. That shit was foul as fuck!"

"You didn't think it was foul while it was happening. You weren't complaining then."

Rocco shook his head at what he'd allowed me to do, unable to look at me. Finally he said, "Look Keema, I need to talk to Treasure. I've gotta get in touch with her. It's important. Can you call her for me?"

I looked at him like he was crazy. He'd just had his dick in my mouth. Now, he was expecting me to call my daughter for him.

"It's important. What just happened will stay between us. But I really need to talk to her," he continued.

"Why the fuck can't *you* call her?"

He paused for a second and closed his eyes. Something was on his mind. A look of uneasiness came across his face as if he had the weight of the world on his shoulders. Something was definitely wrong. He began to massage his temples.

"I told you that I had to turn off my phone. Can you please just do it for me?" he asked.

"What's wrong with your phone? Your fingers broke or something."

"I can't use it."

"Why?"

"Because, I just can't." His patience was being stretched. "I can't tell you why. All you need to know is that I can't use my phone. That's all I can tell you about it." Rocco glanced down at his watch. "Oh shit," he said. "I gotta get this work cooked up."

He quickly grabbed the backpack and headed directly to the kitchen. Reluctantly, I called Treasure. The phone rang several times, but once again, she didn't answer.

"She's not answering," I told him as I wheeled into the

kitchen.

"Try her again."

I sighed, then tried again. Still, there was no answer.

"She's not answering," I said with an irritating pitch.

Even with an arm in a sling, Rocco grabbed a pot from the cabinet, then pulled a couple bricks of raw heroin from the bag, along with two other white powered substances and began to go to work without missing a beat.

"What is that other white stuff?" I questioned like a curious child.

"One is a fever reducin' drug called, Quinine and the other is powered citric acid. I use both to cut the heroin because the Quinine shit is so powerful, it can cause an overdose if I use too much."

"So, are you going to tell me what happened to your arm?"

As Rocco worked the knobs of the stove, he said, "Just some crazy shit."

He left it at that. Seconds later, he placed the heroin into the pot. Over the next several minutes, he stirred the pot and watched it closely while adding the two other ingredients, never taking his eyes off the pot as the drug grew hard.

"Keema, I need your help."

"My help? What do you need my help for?"

"You said earlier that I need somebody to watch my back, right?"

My curiosity was aroused. "Yeah, I did."

"Well, then I need your help."

"What do you need me to do?" I asked.

"You'll see."

"Rocco, I don't like walking into shit blindfolded. I need to know what I'm getting into."

In my head, I saw the deaths of Imani, my mother and Cash. I saw Lucky almost die. I saw the gun in Frenchie's hand as he stood over me just before putting my ass in this damn wheelchair. That was my life and those were consequences I didn't want to ever face again, at least not without knowing exactly what could possibly be coming.

But with all those hurtful memories, there were also the good memories: the nice car I drove, the money I always kept on deck, the good dick I got, the nice clothes I wore. I missed all that terribly. I wanted it all back.

"Keema, I can't tell you. It's that plain and simple. And for now, that's how it's gotta be."

"Alright, well whatever the job is, I need some money up front. I need a cash advance. I need to put some money down to schedule my surgery. I'm tired of waiting and bullshitting."

"How much?"

His eyes were still on the pot.

"Twenty stacks," I told him, knowing the number was steep. But fuck it. Closed mouths don't get fed.

"Alright, I got you."

I was surprised it was that easy. I mean, the nigga didn't negotiate or nothing. He just said okay. Maybe I should've asked for more. At that point, I didn't care what he wanted me to do. I was even willing to risk my probation at that point. Shit, I only had a few more months to go anyway.

He finally took the pot from the stove. "The first thing I need you to do is call my nigga, Ace, and tell 'em to meet me at our normal spot tonight at midnight?"

"Where's the spot?"

"He'll know. Just call, tell 'em exactly that. Tell 'em some shit went down. I really need to get with him about it."

After getting the number, I grabbed my phone and called. Once I gave Ace the message, I hung up and watched as Rocco took a seat at the kitchen table and started to measure, cut, and bag up the work.

"Wowww, how much is that?" As soon as his back was turned, I was going to stuff some of it in my pockets. He wouldn't notice any of it missing. I had no idea how to sell the shit, but how hard could it be to sell to a dope fiend?

"Keema, yo' chill out with all the fuckin' questions," Rocco advised. "All you need to do is call someone else for me."

"Damn, nigga calm down. Who do you want me to call?"

"Snake's, he's sittin' outside in his car."

"Outside? All this time…why didn't you tell him to come in?"

"Don't worry about that shit, Keema. Just hit up his cell and tell 'em everything's good."

I didn't like the fact that Rocco had some random nigga sitting outside my house like it was under surveillance. Immediately, I thought about Mr. Evans. I hoped Snake hadn't been out there when Mr. Evans stopped by. Once again, after getting the number, I called and gave Snake the message.

"See, this is why I did what I did, Rocco," I said, hanging up.

"What do you mean?"

"Because you need a bitch that's gonna hold you down. I mean, look around. Where's Treasure? Where is she? She isn't anywhere to be found. Does that sound like a ride or die bitch to you? Her man is in here with his arm in a sling; having to bag work on his own while she's out somewhere bullshitting."

Rocco didn't say anything. He just kept working, glancing at his watch every now and then as if in a hurry.

"I swear that girl doesn't know how to handle business. I was supposed to have been out of this fucking chair a long time ago, but she keeps giving me the run around. She was even supposed to order me a special car to drive around in. The wench never even did that. All she thinks about is herself."

Rocco was still focused.

"That's why I did what I did for you, Rocco. I knew you needed a real woman on your team. Treasure is still too damn childish to know how to handle shit for you. If she wasn't, she'd be here right now," I added.

"Here," he finally said, pulling out a thick stack of hundred dollar bills from the bag and tossing it on the table. My eyes lit up at the sight.

"That's fifteen stacks right there."

I grabbed the money and looked at it as if I wasn't sure it was real. It had been so long since I'd held that kind of money in my hand.

"I'll hit you with more later," he told me, then shoved the backpack underneath the table. "Gotta make sure you're gonna earn it."

"Trust me, I will."

Immediately, I wondered how much more money was in the bag underneath the table. Why couldn't he give me the whole twenty? I knew he had it. The bag was probably filled with money. My mind drifted to Mr. Evans. I knew the bag had more money in it. There was no doubt. Rocco was just being cautious. I'd been around enough hustlers in my life to know that they never tipped their hand, at least they weren't supposed to. Of course, he wasn't going to tell me how much money was in that bag, but I needed to know. I *had* to know.

I thought about dipping off into another room and calling Mr. Evans. This was my chance. But without knowing exactly how much money was in the bag, it could've been a disaster. Mr. Evans wanted one hundred thousand dollars, not a penny less. Even if Rocco could go get the money, Mr. Evans said he didn't want any surprises.

I also wanted that money for myself. It felt like I was going to hyperventilate. My eyes traveled from Rocco to the bag over and over again. I couldn't be patient. I couldn't wait anymore to find out what my future held. Fuck that! It was time to get this train in motion. It was time to get my ass up out of this damn chair.

"Rocco, there's something I need to tell you."

"What's that?"

"Treasure truly wasn't watching your back."

He looked at me. "What do you mean by that?"

"I know someone who's trying to set you up; they're trying to rob you."

Rocco's eyes increased. "What?"

"Yeah, and this is the type of shit that Treasure should've seen coming. I told you, you need a woman by your side, not a little girl."

"Damn, guess I underestimated you, Keema."

"Guess you did."

He leaned forward in his chair and placed a small, soft peck on my lips. "So, tell me, who's ready to die?"

Chapter 10-
Treasure

"Where the fuck is he?" Toy screamed with the .9mm in her hand. "Start talkin', bitch!"

"I don't know," Maya whimpered with tearful eyes and fear written all over her entire face. "I don't know."

Maya sat on the edge of her bed holding her eight-year-old son in her arms. Both mother and son were crying hysterically as they clung to each other for dear life. Maya's chin rested on her baby's head as she kept his face buried in her chest, not wanting him to see exactly what was going on. Hearing the shouting and cursing was frightening enough. She was trying to shield him as best she could.

"You a muthafuckin' lie!" Toy told her.

"No, I'm not! I swear I'm not! I don't know where Vegas is!"

Tears mixed with mascara ran from Maya's eyes leaving thick black streaks running down her cheeks.

"Bitch, I'm losin' my patience with your dumb ass! You're gonna make me kill you up in here!" Toy ranted.

"Just tell her where he is so we can get this over with," I chimed in.

"I don't know anything. I swear I don't. Please, let me and my son go. Don't hurt us. I promise I won't tell the cops."

"Bitch, fuck you and your damn son!" Toy yelled.

Hearing such heartless words made Maya cry even harder and become more hysterical. Her body shook as she held her son tighter to her body.

"If you cared about your son, you wouldn't be sittin' here tryin' to protect his no good, raping ass daddy," Toy continued.

As sweat ran from Maya's forehead, I could tell she'd never been so scared or nervous before in her life. Plus, the terrifying look on her face said that Maya knew their lives were about to come to an end.

Fed up, Toy charged towards Maya and pressed the nozzle of the gun against her head so hard, she almost fell on the floor.

"Oh God, no!" Maya screamed, squeezing her son tighter and closing her eyes at the feel of the .9mm's cold steel pressed against her skull.

"Treasure, I'm tired of her lyin' ass!" Toy yelled to me as her finger stayed snugly around the trigger, ready to squeeze. I wasn't sure if Toy had it in her to kill, but I'd never seen her this mad.

I'd been pacing the floor endlessly, growing more and more pissed off myself. My patience was wearing super thin with this bitch, too. Just the sound of her voice was starting to irk me.

"Maya, stop playing and just tell us where Vegas is!" I demanded

"I don't…"

Before she could finish her sentence, I charged across the bedroom, and snatched Maya by the collar of her shirt.

"Mommy!" her son screamed.

Toy grabbed him.

Without hesitation, I backhanded Maya across the face so hard her knees buckled and blood flew from her nose across the room. She fell to the floor. "Do you think I'm playing with you?" I yelled, snatching her up by the collar again.

"Mommy!" the little boy screamed again, trying his hardest to break free from Toy's grip but couldn't.

He fought and kicked with all his strength while tears fell from his eyes. Seeing his mother hurt was probably the most frightening thing he'd ever witnessed.

Still gripping her collar and anxious to hit her again, I screamed, "Do you think we're playing? Do you?"

Maya shook her head back and forth in a daze. "No."

I was pretty sure she was seeing double by now. I'd put everything I had into that slap.

"Then where is he?"

"I kicked him out of the house. I haven't seen him since. I..."

I punched Maya in the face as hard as I could once again. I was trying to destroy her beauty. I wanted her to remember this ass whooping forever if she happened to survive this moment. Every time she looked in the mirror, I wanted her to see a reminder of me. I wanted her to get a glimpse into what it felt like to be violated like her husband had done to me.

"Leave my mommy alone!" her son yelled.

Blood poured from Maya's mouth, pooled down her chin and stained her shirt. She swayed drunkenly. "It's okay, Jaden. Mommy's fine," she managed to say.

"Bitch, we can do this shit all night," I barked.

Maya didn't respond. Instead, she just cried. I'm sure in her heart she wished she'd never met Vegas. She'd wished she'd never allowed him to become a part of her life.

I let loose with a strong stomp to her stomach making Maya pull her knees up to her chest and cough. Feeling no remorse, I sent another kick to her ribs, making her curl into a tighter ball as she turned onto her side. Holding her stomach, she threw up on the floor.

"Mommy!" her son screamed again.

"Is this what you want? Do you want your son to see you like this?" I questioned.

Maya was still crying and holding her battered ribs and stomach as she painfully wriggled around in her vomit. "Please," she finally managed to plead. "Whatever Vegas did to you, it has nothing to do with us. Please, you can kill me. You can do whatever you want to me. Just let my son go. I'm begging you."

"Whatever Vegas did to me?" I asked, looking at her like she'd lost her common sense. "Whatever he did to me?"

My nostrils still smelled his cheap cologne. My pores still reeked of his sweat. My pussy still felt him forcing his way inside of me. I could still feel his hands holding me down. It pissed me off so badly I kicked her again.

"Whatever he did to me?" I screamed as the blow landed.

The little boy was hysterical as he tried once again to break free.

"That son of a bitch raped me!"

I let loose with another kick, wishing it was Vegas.

"Stop...please stop! I'm sorry that he did that to you. I'm sorry!" Maya screamed.

"Oh yeah? Are you sorry that he murdered her man, too?" Toy added.

Maya couldn't cry hard enough. Hearing how much of a savage her husband was obviously broke her heart. I'm sure she'd known all along that he was cheating with other women, but apparently never suspected he was coldhearted enough to rape and kill someone. Who would ever expect that their husband was the devil himself?

Once again, I kicked her as if she was Vegas. If I couldn't hurt him, the next best thing was to hurt someone close to him. Every punch, slap and kick felt good to me. The feel of her body beneath my feet and hands felt better than good dick. But none of it would vindicate me. None of it would take the pain away from my heart. Only one thing would do that. I looked over at Maya's son. Within seconds, I stormed across the room, snatched the gun from Toy's hand and placed it to Jaden's head, causing him to look at me with wide innocent eyes.

"Please, don't do this!" Maya screamed frantically from the floor. "Please, I'll do whatever you want!"

"I want Vegas! I want his ass right now or I'll blow this little bastard's head all over this room!"

I'd killed before. Shooting Rick appeared in my memory. I'll never forget that moment for as long as I live. I truly realized how important it was to leave childish things behind at that point. I became a woman that day.

I remember how it felt. I remember the kick of the gun after pulling the trigger. The sound of the explosion still made my ears ring. I could still see the look on Rick's face as he lay on the floor dying, the surprise in his eyes that I'd shot him, gasping for air as he clutched his bleeding chest. I was sure I could do it again. I was sure I could kill again.

Maya got to her knees and raised her hands, scared to death of losing her only child. "I don't know where he is, but I'll call him. I'll call him right now." The words fell from her mouth rapidly.

Toy glanced at me and then back at Maya. She knew my past, but from the look on her face, I think she wondered if I had it in me to kill again, especially to kill a child.

"Where's your cell phone?" I asked Maya.

"In my purse." She pointed towards the nightstand.

Keeping a hold of her son, I made my way to the nightstand and looked inside the purse. After shoving him across the room to Toy, I grabbed the phone. There was also a Bank of America envelope inside. I opened it to see a fat stack of fifties and hundreds. I had no idea what it was for, but it was mine now. I stuffed it in my back pocket before tossing her the phone.

"Please, let my baby go. He's all I've got. Don't hurt him. Please, just let him go," Maya begged.

"Blah, blah, blah, bitch, cry me a damn river," I told her, not giving a flying fuck about her or her son. "You're going to call that rapist ass husband of yours and tell him to come home. Do you understand me?"

She nodded.

"Tell him you're son's hurt and that he needs to get here right away; not a word more, not a word less."

Maya nodded again.

"Well, what the fuck are you waiting on? Get to dialing!" I belted.

With trembling fingers, Maya did as she was told.

In silence, me and Toy watched her and listened, waiting for Vegas to answer the phone. After several moments, he finally did. I immediately placed the nozzle of the gun to the little boy's head again, just in case Maya wasn't too good with following directions.

"Vegas, Jaden hurt himself," she stated frantically. "I don't know what to do. He's hurt bad. Oh God, get here now!"

He attempted to say something, but she interrupted him. "I don't care if you're in D.C. doing something important. Just get here and see about your damn son, Vegas!" Maya screamed, then hung up.

I nodded approvingly and smiled.

"Now, what do we do?" she asked.

I smiled as if she should've already known the answer. "We wait."

Chapter 11-

Keema

My mind consumed a million thoughts per second. I was now so close to walking again I could touch it, I could smell it, I could taste it. The past couple years had seemed like eternity. They'd been torment, torture and pain. Finally, though, the torture was about to come to an end. Finally, I was gonna be able to walk again very soon.

From the passenger seat of the Escalade, I watched the outside world pass by impatiently as Rocco's friend, Snake drove. In the backseat I could hear Rocco, his other homeboy Ace and another dude loading their guns. The interior was filled with thick and constant weed smoke as they each took a hit of a blunt and kept it in rotation.

"Can I have a gun, Rocco?" I asked, turning in my seat.

I knew all hell was gonna break loose when we got to Mr. Evans' store. The last thing I wanted was to be there unarmed. Plus, it wasn't like I could get out the truck and fucking run.

Before Rocco could answer, Snake asked him, "Bruh, why did we bring her? Why we even trustin' her? Since when do we go out and bang on niggas behind something a bitch says?"

"Who you calling a bitch?" I asked, pissed off. Looking at his ugly ass, I could see where he got the name from. He had a big ass head, thick, bushy eyebrows, beady eyes, and dark cratered skin that could've used a trip to the Dermatologist.

"Your crippled ass," Snake responded boldly.

Rocco's other goons couldn't help but laugh.

"Snake, chill out, nigga," Rocco said, still loading bullets into the clip of his gun. "Show her some respect. She's one of us now."

"Man, you know bitches lie."

"Yo' don't worry about it. I can handle it," Rocco answered.

"Shit's gonna get heavy in there, Rocco. Blood's gonna spill. Niggas are gonna get killed. The last thing we need is a witness," Snake added.

"Nigga, will you stop bitching!" I yelled.

Snake looked at me for a quick second before turning back towards the road. "You know, you talk a lot of shit for somebody who can't fuckin' walk."

"Yo' shut the fuck up. I said don't worry about it!" Rocco responded.

Snake shook his head for a few seconds, but just couldn't follow his boss' orders. "Man, I don't feel right about her being here."

"Did I ask yo' ass how you felt about it?" Rocco shouted angrily. "Do I pay you to feel shit?"

Snake glanced at me with untrusting eyes. I didn't like him, and apparently he didn't like me either. I could tell he could possibly see through me. He could probably see how sheisty I really was. He didn't answer Rocco. He just shook his head and continued driving.

"Just drive and be prepared to bang out when we get there, Snake. That's what I'm payin' you for," Rocco added.

"Rocco, baby, I just want to make sure I do my part to hold you down while you're in there," I said. "The last thing I want to see is you get hurt. Just like I told you back at my house, you need a woman to hold you down."

I was laying the shit on super thick, trying to earn his trust.

"Don't worry, Keema, I got this. That nigga is gonna be sorry he ever tried to set me up. He's gonna be sorry he ever spoke my name," Rocco replied. "I'm just glad your homegirl told you what was up. I'm just glad she overheard them niggas plannin' this shit. What's her name again?"

I swallowed the lump in my throat. "Naomi." I hated to involve the girl who worked in the store, but I had to lie on somebody.

Snake glanced at me again. I swear, I couldn't stand him or the sideways ass looks he kept giving me.

The drive seemed like forever. The closer we got to the store the faster and harder my heart thumped. It was about to go down. When we finally reached my old neighborhood, anticipation filled me even more. I began to rub my thighs eagerly. I couldn't wait to get the hit over with.

I knew we'd be able to catch Mr. Evans off guard. He'd never see this coming. I knew he'd figured I was too scared of him to turn the tables on his old ass. Well, he was going to be in for a rude awakening. I couldn't wait to see the look on his frail face when he saw me. He was going to see how it felt to be scared.

"This is the street," I told Snake as we approached an upcoming corner.

Snake slowed as he got to the corner and turned. I was so anxious for the shit to go down, I could barely sit still. I couldn't wait for the festivities to begin.

I pointed. "That's the store."

Snake pulled over to the curb about a block away. He then put the truck in park, turned off the engine and pulled a gun from beneath his seat. "Stay your ass in the truck," he said, reaching for the handle of his door.

"Nah, she's comin' inside with us," Rocco told him.

"What?"

"She's comin' with us," Rocco repeated.

Snake frowned. "Man, are you serious? This crippled bitch is gonna hold us up."

"If you call me one more damn bitch, I swear…"

"What you gon' do? Roll over my big toe?" Snake countered.

The goons laughed again as my eyes glared at him.

"Yo' both of y'all chill the fuck out. Snake, she's goin' in with us, so get her chair out the back," Rocco demanded.

Snake shook his head and mumbled something under his breath.

Moments later, Rocco lifted me out of the passenger seat and placed me into my wheelchair.

"I hope you don't think I'm pushin' yo' ass," Snake told me.

"The chair's electric, idiot," I fired back. "I don't need you. I can push myself."

"Well, just don't get in my way in there. Because if I got to flip you and that muthfuckin' chair over to get up out of there, so be it."

I rolled my eyes. "Fuck you, Snake."

Moments later, we all marched down the sidewalk and into the store like gangbangers. That's when Naomi immediately looked up from reading a magazine and gave me a weird look. "Hey, Keema, what are you doing here?"

Before I could answer her, Rocco's goon, Ace quickly walked around the counter and punched her in the eye so hard she went down like a sack of potatoes. He then snatched Naomi up by her ponytail and led her to the back door on wobbly legs. We all followed.

"Open the door," Ace whispered.

"Please don't kill me," she pleaded in a hushed tone. "I got five kids at home."

Ace yanked her brutally by the head. "Bitch, did I ask for your life story? I said open the damn door."

Everyone had their guns out as Naomi did what she was told. As soon as she opened the door, Ace used her for a shield as each of us rushed inside the room. Mr. Evans and his two goons were caught totally off guard.

"Reach for anything and y'all some dead muthafuckas!" Rocco yelled.

Seeing me, Mr. Evans said from behind his desk, "Bitch, what the fuck is going on here?"

I didn't answer him. Didn't exactly know what to say.

"I asked you a muthafucking question, girl!" Mr. Evans belted at me. He then looked at Rocco and turned his head like he was trying to get a better look. "Hey, aren't you that Atkins boy?" Rocco never said a word. "Yeah, I'm sure you are. Your dad was a legend in the game. Why are you doing this?"

Rocco stepped forward. "Yo', don't bring my pops into this shit. All we need to discuss is why you tryin' to set me up, muthafucka."

Mr. Evans' eyes grew large, realizing who Rocco was. Looking at me, he said, "You double crossing bitch!"

"I told Naomi that I wasn't gonna let this happen." The lies flew from my mouth boldly. "She told me everything about how you were planning to rob Rocco. She told me how you needed the money to keep this old ass store going."

This time Naomi's eyes widened once Mr. Evans looked at her. She was so shocked, she couldn't speak.

"You snake ass bitch! You're lying," Mr. Evans said to me.

"Why would I lie? Besides, it's not like I can rob him? I'm in a fucking wheelchair," I replied in an innocent manner.

"So, you were gonna gut me like a fish?" Rocco said to Mr. Evans, repeating a lie I'd fed him back at the house.

"What?" Mr. Evans said, looking back and forth from Rocco to me.

"Here's your chance, nigga. Here I am. I'm ready to be gutted."

Mr. Evans' two gunmen were silent the entire time. They knew not to make any sudden movements. Trying to reach for their guns would get them shot immediately.

"What you waiting on, nigga?" Rocco continued.

Mr. Evans' face was twisted with fury. His eyes dropped from Rocco to me. They spoke to mine silently. He wanted revenge. He wanted my throat. He wanted my blood. Suddenly, the anger disappeared from his face. His lips curled into a sneer as I displayed a deceitful smirk.

"Somethin' funny?" Rocco asked. "You got somethin' you wanna laugh about before we kill you in here?"

Mr. Evans continued to sneer. I didn't like it. The shit looked creepy. Suddenly, each of us was caught off guard by what happened next.

BOOM!!!

An explosion came from out of nowhere, ripping a hole through the front of the desk. Immediately, Naomi's stomach exploded as a slug from Mr. Evans' hidden shotgun tore into her. The slug had such force it went directly through the girl's body and tore into Ace, who was holding her from behind. He was lifted off his feet and thrown back a few yards to the floor. With his eyes wide open, he died upon impact.

At that point, all hell broke loose.

Mr. Evans' goons reached for their guns and started shooting. Rocco and his boys returned fire. Bullets were flying in all directions. It looked like some shit out of a Quentin Tarantino movie.

"Oh my God!" I screamed with wide eyes, not knowing what else to do.

"Muthafucka!" Mr. Evans shouted as he let off another cannon like explosion from his shotgun.

Rocco ducked to the floor, then hastily snatched me from my wheelchair and down with him as everyone else took cover. I could hear bullet after bullet whiz by my ear. I could hear them tearing into walls and furniture. Thinking I was about to die once again, I buried my face and immediately started praying.

"Die, muthafuckas!" Mr. Evans screamed, bussing shot after shot.

"Fuck you!" Rocco screamed, lying on the floor returning fire.

As Snake ducked behind a couch and let off shots, Mr. Evans' gunmen took cover themselves, returning fire whenever they could. Within seconds, my wheelchair looked like Swiss cheese. It was filled with hundreds of holes. The sight scared me to death, knowing that I'd been sitting in it just moments before. If Rocco hadn't snatched me down when he did, I'd be dead. Glass from an overhead light bulb shattered down on us as a bullet whizzed through it. Plaster from the walls and ceiling fell. The bullets wouldn't stop flying or ripping shit apart.

Oh God, what have I gotten myself into, I thought, pulling myself as close to Rocco as I could.

"Where you at, you double crossing bitch?" Mr. Evans yelled from behind his desk to me. "Lift your head up and let me see it so I can blow it off!"

His shot gun continuously went off, destroying anything in its path.

I covered my ears and closed my eyes tightly. The shots were so loud they had them ringing.

"Come on…where you at? Let me see you!"

Mr. Evans wanted me badly. I opened my eyes just in time to see one of his gunmen who'd taken cover by a pool table catch a bullet through his right eye from Snake's gun. The back of his head exploded on impact. Brain matter splattered behind him as his body fell backwards to the floor. He lay dead in his own blood. My eyes widened at the sight.

The shots wouldn't stop.

Rocco finally ran out of bullets. He quickly reached into his pocket with his one good arm and pulled out another clip. After ejecting the empty one to the floor, he shoved the new one into the butt of his gun and cocked the slide.

"Stay down!" he told me.

He then stood up and aimed directly at Mr. Evans. He squeezed off seven shots. Each ripped directly into the old man's chest, causing his body to shake violently with the entry of each. The force of the bullets knocked his chair back on its heels. He dropped his gun. Seconds later, he fell to the floor. Blood soaked his shirt.

Rocco got down low again. He, Snake, and Rocco's other goon all turned their attention on Mr. Evans' final gunman. They all sent endless shots in his direction as he hid behind a poorly made bar. Bullets tore into the fragile wood over and over again. Moments later, Rocco signaled to his partners to circle around the bar. All three men kept shooting as they made their way across the room towards the gunman's hiding spot. Snake was the first to reach it. He caught the gunman kneeling with his back to him. Even though he was probably already dead, without hesitation, Snake aimed at the back of the gunmen's skull and squeezed the trigger.

"Got his ass!" Snake said.

"Let's get the fuck up out of here!" Rocco yelled. He ran back across the room to me, picked me up and quickly carried me to the door.

Within only seconds, we were balling out of the store and dashing to the truck at top speed. As the truck peeled off down the street, I couldn't help but think about how many times I'd tried to get out of the game. To live a normal life without all the stress and drama, but this shit just kept pulling me back in. It took a tremendous amount of willpower to turn my back on fast cash, and besides retirement was just too fucking boring anyway.

Chapter 12-

Treasure

"Do you know where Heaven is?" I asked Jaden in a soft voice as we sat on the bed.

Jaden didn't answer. He was obviously too terrified to speak.

"It's okay," I assured him. "You can tell me."

He finally nodded.

"Where?"

Pointing towards the ceiling, he said, "It's up there in the sky. You can't see it though because of all the clouds."

"Right," I told him approvingly and with a smile. "That's exactly where it is."

"My mom told me that's where my grandparents are."

Staring at us with red, swollen eyes, Maya looked pitiful as she sat on the floor with a defeated posture and listened to her son.

"Yeah, she's probably right. Do you know how Heaven looks?" I continued.

"Yeah. It's all white and a whole bunch of angels live there. They've got little round things hanging over their heads."

Toy chuckled while chewing the hell out of a piece of gum.

I glanced at Maya again with a wicked smile. "Do you want to go to Heaven, Jaden?"

He nodded.

"Well, I can take you there right now. But there's a problem. Even though Heaven is in the sky, you can't get there by plane."

Uneasiness filled Jaden's expression. Although he was young, he wasn't stupid. He had an idea where this was going.

"What's wrong?" I asked him. "Don't you want to go?" Although my tone was innocent, the sarcasm was clear.

He shook his head and took a step back.

"Why?" I asked.

"Because I would have to die. I don't wanna die."

Maya began whimpering.

"But that's the only way you can get there, sweetie."

"I don't want to," he said, shaking his head. Fear was now written all over his face.

Snatching him by his hand and jerking him towards me like a rag doll, the peaceful look on my face evaporated and the innocent tone of my voice vanished. "Well, if that bitch ass mother of yours is playing games, you won't have a choice in the matter."

Jaden started crying.

"Please," Maya pleaded. "He has nothing to do with…"

"Shut the fuck up!" I yelled, jumping to my feet. "That punk ass excuse for a baby daddy of yours was supposed to have been here by now. It's been over an hour! I don't know what the deal is. But if he ain't here in ten more minutes, I'm gonna give your son a first class ticket to Heaven!"

Maya pleaded even more.

"Shut the fuck up!"

She still attempted.

Smacking her across the face with the butt of the gun, I

screamed, "I said shut the fuck up!"

Curled up on the floor, Maya finally did as she was told. Among the sounds of her whimpers, each of us sat in silence. I continued to hold Jaden close to me while Toy stood over Maya. Repeatedly, I glanced at my watch as minute after minute passed by. My temper grew more with each passing second. Finally, the ten minutes were up.

"I hope you know how fucked up it is that your so called husband never showed up. He never even tried to call back. He ain't shit. Time's up!" I shouted as I snatched Jaden's little scrawny frame off the bed. "I'm blowing his head off."

"No!" Maya screamed as she attempted to get to her feet. "Please don't do this. I'm sure Vegas will be here soon. He said he was in D.C. Maybe he was in a car accident or something. Just let me call him back."

"Fuck that! I told your ass I wasn't playing. I told you this wasn't a game. Obviously you didn't believe me so now it's time to accept the consequences."

Jaden's back was flat against the wall and the tip of my gun was directly at the center of his forehead. Sheer terror was in his eyes as he looked up at me.

"I'll pay you!" Maya screamed. "I can get you money! A whole lot of it! I swear I can!"

Anyone who knows me knows that money is always music to my ears. Money makes me cum. "Speak on it, bitch!" I yelled to her without taking the gun away from Jaden's head or turning around.

"I don't have it," Maya said quickly. "But my cousin does."

When Toy's cell phone rang, she headed off to a nearby corner and answered.

"Where's your cousin?" I questioned.

"I don't know, but I can call her and get you money right now. I swear I can."

I turned to Maya and gave her a skeptical look. I

couldn't be sure if she was bullshitting. She was probably just trying to buy time. It was clear how a person would say just about *anything* to save their own life or the life of their child. I didn't quite trust her.

Sensing my skepticism, she said, "I swear I can get you some money. All I have to do is call her."

"How much?"

"Five grand...maybe ten."

"Oh no bitch, your man owed me twenty, and now since he wants to play games, the price has doubled. I need forty now," I countered.

Maya seemed concerned, but tried not to show it. "Okay."

Against my better judgment, I pulled my phone from my pocket and tossed it to her. "Make the call. And this better not be no bullshit, you understand?"

Maya nodded as she began to dial numbers.

"And talk loud and clear; no codes or whispering." Normally, I would've told her to put the phone on speaker, but I wanted the background to be as quiet as possible.

"No games," Maya assured me as she placed the phone to her ear.

For several moments, I watched her as she waited for her cousin to answer. When she finally did, Maya immediately told her she was in a bind and needed forty thousand dollars.

There was brief silence.

"I can't tell you why," Maya finally said. "It's just real important. Trust me, I'll pay you back. I swear I will."

I watched and listened for anything that didn't look or sound right. I also couldn't help but wonder what her cousin did for a living to have that type of cash. After several more moments, Maya said a few more words and hung up.

"Well?" I asked anxiously.

"She's going to give it to me."

"When?"

"Tomorrow night."

"Tomorrow night? Why can't she give it to you now?"

"Because she's in Hawaii on vacation, and can't make it here before then."

"So, how does she have forty stacks to just give away like that?"

"She has her own business."

I was still skeptical. The shit sounded too good to be true. But before I could ask her another question, Toy ended her call.

"Oh my God Treasure, you're not gonna believe this shit."

"What?" I inquired.

"My homegirl just told me somebody saw Rocco on the West side earlier."

I looked at her in complete disbelief. "You can't be serious."

"I know it sounds crazy, but that's what she said. She also told me word around the hood is that him and his crew got into a shootout with some old dude. And get this…they sayin' that your mother was with them."

I couldn't believe the shit I was hearing.

"Treasure, Rocco is *alive*!" she screamed happily. "Did you hear me? He's alive!"

I didn't know what to say or do. I was excited but in shock at the same time. All I kept thinking was…*my mother…with Rocco. That can't be true.* Finally, I broke out of my daze. "I've gotta go home, and ask my mother what the fuck is going on. Maybe he's at my house."

"But what about these two?" Toy questioned, speaking of Maya and Jaden.

"Well, we can't leave them here, so I need you to take them somewhere safe and keep an eye on them until her cousin shows up. I'm taking your car, so you gotta roll in her shit. "

Toy's face looked displeased. "Why me? Why can't you

take them? And what cousin?"

"Because I gotta go see about Rocco, that's why."

"Treasure…"

"Look, Toy, we're getting ready to make forty thousand dollars off this shit, so I need you to cooperate."

"How?"

"While you were on the phone, I made some shit happen. Her cousin is gonna bring us forty stacks tomorrow night."

Toy's eyes widened.

"Yeah, forty stacks."

"Well, I want twenty, Treasure."

"Twenty?"

"Yeah, twenty. If I'm gonna be kidnappin' muthafuckas, it has to be worth my while."

Greedy bitch, I thought to myself. "Alright girl, you know I got you. We're girls. You know I split everything with you."

She looked at me sideways, then twisted her lips. "Uh-huh, just like you split that money you tucked earlier from Maya's purse?"

Damn, I had no idea she'd seen that.

"Girl, you know I was gonna break bread with you," I lied.

"When?" Toy asked, obviously not believing a word coming out of my mouth.

"Later on."

"Well, fuck all that. I need my cut right now." Her hand was out like a true panhandler.

"Toy, I don't have time to sit here and argue with you over that petty ass money. If you want some real cash, I can hit you off once I get home. I got more money stashed there. Now, I gotta go see about Rocco," I said, heading towards the door.

Once again, Toy looked at me with suspicion.

"Oh, so what…you don't trust me? I thought we were friends."

"Treasure, this is business. Besides, didn't you tell me the other day 'ain't no room for friendship when it comes to money'?"

"Just make sure nothing happens to them," I replied, ignoring her comment. I then handed Toy the gun and headed out of the bedroom towards the front door.

"Get your ass up, bitch," I could hear her ordering Maya. "We got somewhere to be."

As soon as I pulled into the driveway, I immediately hopped out of Toy's car. Knowing my baby was still alive had me anxious beyond words to see him. I needed to touch him, kiss him, smell him. I needed to feel him in my arms. I needed to taste his lips. I prayed to God that if he wasn't inside, my mother could give me some insight on what the hell was going on.

Nearly stumbling up my mother's ramp, I dashed onto the porch and into the house. The living room was empty, but I could hear voices coming from the kitchen. With no hesitation, I charged through the house in that direction. My eyes grew to the size of cantaloupes when I saw my baby standing by the sink with his arm in a sling.

"Rocco!" I screamed as soon as I saw him. I darted across the kitchen floor like the Road Runner and wrapped my arms around his neck.

"Damn, girl, my arm," he said, exposing his gap toothed smile.

"Forget your arm," I replied, punching him in the shoulder. "You had me scared to death. I thought you were dead."

Glancing back at my mother who had her chair rolled under the kitchen table; I could've sworn I caught her rolling her eyes at me. I wondered why she was in an old chair that wasn't electric, but swiftly dismissed the thought.

"Where have you been?" I asked, running my hands

across his dreads, just wanting to touch him all over.

"Look, it's a long story. I had to fall back for a minute and check things out."

"Check things out...Well, I've been calling you. Why was your phone off?"

"I told you I had to fall back. Until I could figure out who I could trust, I wasn't callin' anyone or answerin' any calls, and I still can't. I'll tell you about it later."

"Well, what happened to your arm?"

"Some nigga named Vegas rolled up on me and started blastin' out of no where. I don't even know this dude."

My heart sunk at hearing Vegas' name.

"The muthafucka hit me in the arm, but I still got away. One of my boys took me over to see a friend of his who's a re-tired doctor. For the right price, he'll fix your shit if you've been banged up. He said the bullet went in and out, so I'm good. Luckily, that bitch ass nigga had a small caliber gun."

All I could think about was how Vegas said he'd killed him. "Well, what happened on the West side? People are saying that you were in some kind of shootout and my mother was with you."

"I don't wanna discuss that. But I do wanna discuss why the Vegas nigga kept screamin' about *you* though," Rocco in-formed.

I grew nervous.

"Talk to me, Treasure. How do you know this nigga?"

"Yeah, Treasure, how do you know him?" my mother asked with sarcasm in her voice. "We're listening."

I really didn't want to discuss my personal business in front of her, but I went ahead and told Rocco about the rape. I told him all the details, but purposely left out the part about why Vegas raped me. As I explained, my phone rang. After looking at the screen and realizing that it was Toy, I pressed the ignore button.

"He raped you?" Rocco asked as rage took over his face.

"But why? What beef does he have with you?"

"Yeah, what's the beef, Treasure?" my mother co-signed, folding her arms. "You always into some shit. And this time you almost got your man killed behind it. You can be so dumb sometimes."

"Ma, will you shut up and stay out of this?"

Rocco started to pace the floor like an angry lion in his cage. I could tell he wanted answers.

My phone rang again. It was Toy. I still didn't answer.

"That's the shit I was talking about, Rocco," my mother continued. "Treasure doesn't know what the hell she's doing out here in these streets. She's a damn amateur. And her bullshit is going to get you killed."

"Ma, stay out of this!" I warned again.

"Why? Because you don't want your man to know that you're a child trying to play a grown woman's game?"

"I need to know what the fuck is goin' on when I get back from the bathroom, Treasure," Rocco griped.

He was barely out of ear shot when my mother kept running her mouth.

"Stop trying to play a grown woman's game," she said while shaking her head.

Not in the mood to entertain her ass, I walked out of the kitchen and headed to my bedroom. On the way, a text from Toy came through on my phone.

I ADVISE U NOT TO KEEP IGNORING ME. THIS AIN'T A GAME, TREASURE. I WANT MY MONEY!!

Does this bitch call herself trying to threaten me, I thought to myself.

I couldn't get Toy on the phone fast enough so I could put her ass in check. But when I raised my head after walking into my bedroom, I knew that call would have to wait. When my eyes surveyed the destruction, I stood frozen in the doorway. My eyes scoured the clothes, drawers, shoes and everything else tossed all over the floor. It didn't take a rocket scientist to know who'd done it or what she'd been looking for. I turned on my heels and stormed towards the kitchen. I then stood directly in front of my mother and got right in her face.

"Where the fuck is my money, you sneaky bitch?"

Chapter 13-

My blood boiled as I gazed down at my mother. I could feel my body trembling with something surpassing anger. I was beyond the point of furious. "Where the fuck is it?" I screamed again with both fists clinched.

She shrugged her shoulders nonchalantly. "I don't know what you're talking about. What money?"

Her little laid-back 'I don't give a shit' attitude made me want to snatch her by the neck with both hands and ring it like a Thanksgiving turkey.

"Don't play games with me! Where is my damn money?" I yelled

"I told you I don't know what you're talking about. But I know you better check your damn tone. I'm not one of your friends, Treasure and we're not standing on some street corner. I'm your mother and this is *my* house. Talk to me like you've got some sense or don't talk to me at all."

She attempted to roll away, but I grabbed the chair. "My money was here when I left! Now, it's gone. So are you trying to tell me that my shit just grew legs and walked the fuck off on its own?"

"Look, don't go accusing me, Treasure. I ain't no damn thief," she countered.

"You could've fooled me."

Her eyes narrowed with spite at those words. She was super heated. "You little bitch," she sneered. "I said I didn't take your money. And I don't like being called a liar."

I threw up my hands. "Then where did it go, huh? Where did my money go?"

"How the hell should I know? I was with Rocco. I don't keep up with your shit. Maybe we got robbed."

I fumed even more than before, knowing she was insulting my intelligence. She was trying my patience and now I was only a fraction of an inch away from my breaking point. Fury came over me. Something about her eyes made me want to black both of them. Something about her mouth made me want to make it bloody.

"Ma, I'm not playing with you."

I looked directly into her eyes with a serious stare. I needed her to see that she was seconds away from pushing me over the edge. The last thing I wanted to do was whip a crippled bitch. I swear I didn't, but she was making it hard. She was seriously asking for me to snatch her up out of that damn chair and beat her like a nigga in the street.

"This is your last chance," I warned. "Tell me where my money is or else."

She chuckled, then returned my stare. "Is that a threat?"

"It sure is."

We stared at each other in silence, looking like two rams preparing to collide violently.

Finally, she leaned forward in her chair and said defiantly, "Treasure, fuck you, your money and your weak ass threats. Now, jump if you're bad, bitch."

That was all I needed. My patience snapped at that very

moment like a twig. Unable to hold back, I punched my mother dead in the mouth, instantly splitting her bottom lip. For a moment, she was in shock. She looked at me intently, in complete disbelief. She couldn't wrap her mind around the fact that I'd hit her.

"I told you I wasn't playing! I don't play when it comes to my fucking money!"

Her eyes grew wide with rage. "You bitch!" she screamed and attempted to lunge at me; almost falling out of the chair. I quickly stepped back.

"Yo', what the fuck is goin' on in here?" Rocco yelled entering the kitchen.

"I'm gonna kill this bitch!" my mother screamed, still trying to get near me. When that didn't work, she picked up a fork along with a bottle of ketchup and threw them in my direction.

I had to admit, for someone in a wheelchair, she was a feisty muthafucka, and had a pretty decent aim.

Rocco charged across the kitchen toward us.

Moments later, Shane came into the kitchen, too. "Keema and Treasure fight," he chanted. "Keema and Treasure fight."

"Get out of here, Shane!" my mother demanded.

"Keema suck Rocco…"

Picking up a glass bowl full of grapes, my mother threw it at him like a professional pitcher, sending the fruit in several different directions. Extremely slow to react, the bowl hit Shane on the arm.

"I said get your fat ass out of here!" she ranted.

"What did you just say, Shane?" I asked curiously. Even Rocco displayed a weird expression.

"Keema mad…Keema throw a bowl at Shane," he stated. "Keema mad."

"Get out of here now, damnit!" my mother roared.

Shane finally did as he was told.

"Why did you do that to him?" I shouted.

Rocco stood between us. "Treasure, you need to calm down. This shit is gettin' outta hand."

Before I could respond, I watched as my mother wheeled over to the sink, snatched open a drawer and grabbed a butcher knife. "You think this shit is a game. I'm about to kill your ass! You accuse me of being a thief, then you turn around and put your hands on me. Nahhh, tramp, it's about to be some repercussions up in here! Don't let this fucking wheelchair fool you!"

Rocco held out his hand. "Yo', Keema, put the knife down."

I had to admit, I was a bit nervous because I know how crazy my mother could get, but I wasn't about to back down. "I just want my damn money!"

"I told you I ain't got your money! I work for Rocco now. I don't need to steal no money from you!" she ranted.

I looked from her to Rocco. "What is she talking about, Rocco? What does she mean she works for you?"

"Chill," he said.

"No, fuck that. What is she talking about?" I asked again.

"Calm down, Treasure. I'm puttin' *you* in charge of her, so I'm gonna need you to keep a level head," he answered.

"What the fuck do you mean you're putting her in charge of me?" my mother questioned.

"Look, both of y'all need to calm the fuck down. When y'all do that, we can talk about gettin' this money," Rocco added.

"Fuck that, Rocco! You're not putting that bitch over me! I was the one who held you down today, remember? Now you're putting her over me? Are you crazy?" my mother belted.

I displayed a conniving grin. "Yeah, now what. I'ma boss around this muthafucka!"

My mother's face twisted up with pure evil at those

words. Gripping the handle of the knife, she said, "Rocco, you got two seconds to get that bitch out of my face before I kill her."

"Keema…" Rocco said slowly.

"Get her out of here, *now!*"

Knowing she was serious, Rocco grabbed my hand and led me to the front door, telling me we needed to go somewhere to talk.

Rocco stroked his thick dick up inside me like his life depended on it. His sex game was always good, but tonight he worked my pussy like it was on punishment. I wasn't a screamer, but he had my ass damn near hoarse. I'm sure our hotel neighbors were either turned on or pissed off.

"You're killing my pussy!" I screamed, enjoying both the pleasure and pain.

Rocco didn't respond with words, only more strokes.

We'd already been going at it for nearly an hour. I was winded, but Rocco wasn't easing up. He'd already made me cum three times and seemed to be determined to make me cum again. He even made me squirt twice. That shit tripped me out. I'd never squirted before. I'd heard of it and seen white bitches do it in porn movies, but I'd never done it before. The feeling was ten times better than a regular orgasm. It was extreme and the feeling was just that intense.

"Oh God, Rocco!" I moaned. "Give it to me, daddy!"

Rocco obliged. He gave it to me hard and deep as I grinded my hips upward then wrapped my thighs around him and locked my ankles.

"Yes, Rocco, yes!"

Finally, Rocco couldn't hold back anymore. With a gut wrenching grunt, he released a thick load of sperm inside of me before collapsing on top of my breasts. With his dick still in-side, I held him in my arms, knowing he was drained. After several minutes, he rolled off of me. As he lay on his back, I curled up beside him, rested my head on his chest and began to softly trace his RIP tattoo with my index finger. It was surrounded by two angel wings, a heart and a date.

I'd asked on several occasions who the tattoo was for since there wasn't a name attached, but he always said the same thing, 'someone very special'. He never discussed it any further; like it wasn't any of my business, so I eventually stopped asking. That was the one thing I hated about Rocco. He was too damn secretive, and our conversations were always on a need to know basis. The only thing I knew about him was that his mother had died of ovarian cancer when he was ten, and that he had two younger sisters who lived with his aunt in Towson.

Apparently, he hated his aunt and wasn't very close to his family which might've explained why he was so distant sometimes. To make matters worse, in the eight months that we'd been dating, I'd only gone to one of his boy's house or a hotel to chill, fuck or hang out. My only hope was that one day he would trust me enough to open up.

"So, where did all that come from?" I asked him, speaking of the sex.

"Had to release some stress," he responded with a sexy smile.

"Well, you should be nice and calm now," I joked.

Rocco rubbed my head a few times. "I've been thinkin'. You know you need to take yo' ass back to school."

He sounded just like a father. Normally, I would've told the average person to stay the fuck out of my business, but not Rocco. For some reason, I wanted him to be proud of me.

"Yeah, I know. And I'm gonna go back. It's not like I've been out the whole year." Hopefully that lie would satisfy him for now because actually I'd been considering dropping out for good. I didn't have time for that shit. There was money to be made.

We laid in silence for a moment until my phone started

vibrating on the desk. It had been ringing every fifteen to twenty minutes, and I knew exactly who it was…Toy. However, I ignored it just like all the other calls. But if that bitch thought she was gonna send me a threatening text message and get away with it, she was sadly mistaken. I was just waiting to blast her ass when Rocco wasn't around. Even Rasheeda had called, but I didn't answer her call either. I was with my man, so everybody had to wait.

"Why do you want my mother to work for you?" I asked Rocco once the phone stopped. "I'm really not trying to share you with her."

"Because she's a soldier," he replied. "And I'm always lookin' to recruit good talent."

"I guess. But shit, how much can a crippled bitch do?"

"You'd be surprised. Besides, this will help boost her self-esteem. Isn't that what you wanted? You're always sayin' she needs to quit feelin' sorry for herself, right?"

"Yeah," I grumbled. "But damn."

"Trust me, it's gonna work out," he responded with confidence. "Besides, it looks like she needs the money for some type of surgery. She told me that she asked you for the dough, but you been shittin' on her. What's up with that?"

I chuckled. "Her dumb ass doesn't even know if that surgery is really gonna work. I mean come on…she found out about the shit over the internet. And it's not even done in the United States."

"Well, I guess she's just willin' to try anything at this point. Shit, I don't blame her."

I paused for a second. "Honestly, Rocco I just don't want her to be happy."

He looked at me with wide eyes. "Are you serious?"

"Absolutely. If you only knew half the shit my mother put me through you would understand why I feel this way. That bitch truly messed my childhood up, so she doesn't deserve any money for that surgery. She needs to suffer…just like I did."

"Damn. I didn't know it was like that."

"Well, it's a lot of shit you don't know about her. Like the fact that she's a fucking thief. And since you decided to hire her without getting a background check, I would be careful."

Rocco smiled for the second time, this time there was more to his smile. Something I couldn't put my finger on. "I can handle it."

"I hope so."

"Hey listen, it's somethin' that you need to know."

I stared at him. "What is it?"

"I turned my phone off because I think my shit is tapped. And I'm not sure what's up, but I need to stay on my toes so I'm gettin' rid of it."

A tapped phone came with the territory due to the business he was in, so I wasn't shocked. But, I was surprised that he'd finally shared something with me.

"Well, thanks for letting me know. I understand that you had to be extra careful."

Before Rocco could respond, my phone vibrated again. I ignored it.

"Who keeps callin' you, and why don't you answer? You scared yo' shit might be tapped, too?" he joked.

"No, it's just Toy."

"So, why don't you answer?"

I paused for a moment, not sure if I should tell him what was going on.

Sensing my hesitation, he looked down at me. "Treasure, what's up?"

I went ahead and told him about the Maya situation. I told him everything, except the part about Maya calling her cousin for money.

"Kidnappin', Treasure?" Rocco asked me like I was crazy as he immediately sat up in bed.

"Baby, I didn't know what else to do. You wouldn't answer your phone. I thought Vegas had killed you. There was no damn way I was gonna let him get away with that. His ass was going to pay."

"Do you know how serious this shit is, especially with a kid involved?"

"Yeah, but it's too late now. There's no going back. Maya knows my face. She knows who I am."

Rocco shook his head like a disappointed parent. "Damn, Treasure."

"I know, but what else could I do?"

He was quiet for a moment, letting everything sink in. "This could turn out real bad."

"Look, as long as I've got Maya and her son, we can get Vegas back."

"But I was gonna handle that nigga in my own way. You didn't need to get involved," he badgered. "Now, we're gonna have to handle Maya and her son, too. Treasure, that's a triple homicide. Niggas go to the chair for shit like that."

Damn, he was right. I'd never truly thought about all that. Through my thirst for revenge, I didn't quite think about what could happen down the line.

"Not only that," Rocco continued. "How well do you trust Toy?"

"What do you mean?"

"If she gets caught, she might tell everything just to save her own ass."

"But she'll be looking at prison just like us," I replied.

"Not if she cooperates with the police. They'll give her a lighter sentence. Shit, if she tells them enough, she might not have to do a bid at all."

I hadn't thought about that either. Now, I was stressing. I didn't know what to do. I couldn't let Maya and her son go. They knew who I was. They'd go to the cops for sure. But if I killed them, I would now have to kill Toy too just to ensure that she didn't fuck around and turn on me somewhere down the line. This shit was crazy.

My phone vibrated again. This time I jumped up and snatched it from the desk, looking at the screen. Sure enough, it was Toy.

"She's just gonna keep callin'," Rocco said. "Plus, it might be somethin' real important. Answer."

He was right. "Hello."

"So, now you know how to answer your damn phone, huh?" Toy belted.

"Look, calm down. I had to handle something. Anyway, how's everything with Maya and the kid."

"Oh, so now you're worried about them?"

Her attitude was annoying me. "Toy, I just told you I was busy. Now, stop tripping. How's everything going with them?"

"There is no *them*."

I didn't like the way that sounded, at all. I pressed the phone tighter to my ear than before, needing to hear everything she said from that point clearly.

"Toy, what do you mean there is no *them*?"

"Exactly what I just said."

My heart started to beat like a drum.

"You thought you were slick," she said. "You thought you were going to pawn Maya and the kid off on me and leave me holding the bag for your sneaky ass. That's why you wouldn't answer your phone."

"Toy, what are you talking about? What did you do?"

"I see right through you, Treasure. You're not loyal. You've never been. All you do is use people."

"Toy, what did you do?" I reiterated.

"I let both of them go."

The words rained down on me like a ton of bricks. In my mind, all I could see was Maya headed directly to the police station at that very moment.

Damn.

Chapter 14-

As he pushed himself inside me over and over again with absolutely no rhythm, the sound of shrieking bedsprings beneath me seemed like the loudest sound I'd ever heard in my life. They were as annoying and loud as nails sharply making their way down the entire length of a chalkboard. The sound of the young man's pleasure filled moans were also more of a torment than anything else.

My nostrils were also being assaulted mercilessly by the scent radiating from his naked body. It was making me so nauseous, I almost gagged several times. The combination of his breath and sweat was making it even worse. God, I swear it was taking everything inside of me to keep my dinner down. I could feel my stomach fighting against the urge to vomit as it turned over and over again.

My eyes were closed. They'd been that way since he first began to fuck me. Although he was slightly handsome, I couldn't bear to look at him. I definitely couldn't look into his eyes. I didn't want to see him. I didn't want to see his chubby body. My eyes preferred the darkness behind my eyelids.

My hands couldn't find it in themselves to touch him. They couldn't find it in themselves to grab his hips and pull him deeper into me. My fingernails had no interest whatsoever in digging into his back.

It had been so long since I'd fucked. It had been so long since I'd had a dick inside of me. Even though I could only feel pressure, my body yearned for sex like air, water and food. So obviously, now that I was finally getting some, I should've at least tried to enjoy it. My pussy should've been jumping for joy. Instead, it was the most disgusting moment I'd ever been a part of. It was horrible.

As he grunted and moaned loudly with each stroke, I detached myself from the moment as best I could. I wanted it over. Detaching myself from the moment was the only way I could escape. But until it was over, all I could do was try to think about a million other things that had absolutely nothing to do with the situation. I felt like a child being molested.

Finally, with one final thrust, Shane released his load into the condom covering his dick. As he let loose, he gave off a screeching groan and his body stiffened. Within another second, he collapsed on top of me. Immediately, I pushed him off. Giving him some pussy in the first place was bad enough. The last thing I could take right now was cuddling with him.

Guilt and shame immediately came over me. How could I have done this? How could I have let it happen? How could I have even entertained the thought of allowing it to happen in the first place? I was disgusted with myself; so disgusted that instead of letting him lay beside me, I said, "Shane, put your clothes on and go."

"Did Shane hurt you?" he asked innocently.

"Shane, just get out, okay? I don't wanna talk."

I needed him gone. I couldn't take facing him for another moment. I'd only given him some pussy to keep him quiet about what he'd seen between me and Rocco. With things going so well, the last thing I needed was Shane fucking things up for me.

Shane got up and took the rubber off. After tossing it in the trash, he got dressed and left.

"And remember!" I shouted to him. "This is our secret. Don't tell anyone!"

In his absence, all I could do was lay in the darkness of my bedroom and stare at the ceiling in silence. Wanting to walk had broken me down. It had made me desperate. It had me selling my soul to the damn devil. I hated who I was becoming, but I couldn't help it. I needed to walk again. Nothing or no one meant more. I needed a cigarette. Grabbing the Newport pack, I quickly pulled one out and lit it up. I'd only put it to my lips twice before my cell phone rang.

When I grabbed it and saw Snake's name and number on the screen, I answered. "Yeah, what's up?"

"I'm ready," he said.

Knowing what we had to do, I said, "Alright, I'll be at your house in a minute," and hung up the phone.

Without hesitation, I maneuvered myself out of bed into my wheelchair. Twenty minutes later, I was dressed, and wheeling myself down the ramp in front of my house.

Two days had blown by since me and Treasure got into that huge fight. She hadn't even been back home or called, which was probably for the best. I was still pissed at her ass for hitting me, and instead of dwelling on it, I simply put it out of my head and kept things moving. Right now, life for me was taking a few steps ahead. In just two short days, I was starting to find a little happiness.

As I leaned back into the driver's seat of my brand new caravan, it felt good to maneuver through the traffic and the streets again. I loved the feel of the steering wheel in my hand. It had been so long since I'd driven a car and I missed the shit out of it. I missed a lot of small things like that.

Although the used, handicapped-equipped caravan wasn't quite my style, and it wasn't fly like my Camero, the fact that I'd taken the money that I stole from Treasure along with some of the money that Rocco gave me and paid cash for it, made up for everything. I was so proud of myself. I was even more proud that it only took me six hours to learn how to drive the modified vehicle.

Of course, my instructor told me that I had to reapply for a restricted driver's license, along with some other bullshit that would take a while, but I didn't have time for that. I had to make some moves. As long as I'd gone without having independence, I could care less about driving without a license. It felt good to have accomplished something. I still needed help occasionally getting in and out of the van, but it didn't faze me or put a damper on my happiness. But what felt even better was realizing that I was one step closer to walking again.

Along with sending Ms. Kyle some money for Deniro, I'd contacted the doctor in The Dominican Republic and the two of us began to seriously talk about making preparations for the surgery. He even told me that it was best that I stopped smoking, which I didn't have a problem with. Whatever it took to make this shit happen, I was more than willing to do.

Since I'd purchased the car, I needed to come up with a few more thousand for my deposit, but the way things were going, I knew I'd have the twenty-five thousand sooner than expected. With things finally moving in the direction, it was only a matter of time before I was finally out of that damn wheelchair. All I had to do was stay on Rocco's good side.

Since the Mr. Evans shooting, Rocco had really been fucking with me hard. He'd given me a job just like he'd said he would and obviously trusted me. As long as things continued to work out between me and him, the surgery was pretty much written in stone.

He didn't know it, but I had serious plans for Rocco.

Once this whole surgery shit was over, and I recovered, I was gonna go super hard at taking him away from Treasure. Fuck her. She really didn't know what she had in Rocco. She couldn't handle a nigga like him. He needed a queen, not a princess. Once I could walk again, manipulating him would be easy. I'd throw it on him so good he'd forget all about Treasure's young ass.

Maybe it was wrong, but Treasure had brought this on herself. Putting her hands on me was the worst thing she could've ever done. That, combined with my surgery money never being a top priority for her, had made things this way. I now saw her the way I see other bitches out in the street. There would be revenge. I promised that to myself. I wasn't quite sure how I'd get it besides taking Rocco from her. But whatever it would be, it was going to be crucial.

Several minutes later, I finally approached the corner of Snake's street. After making a left turn, I pulled up to the curb in front of his house and blew the horn. Moments later, his front door opened and he came out with a camouflage backpack dangling from his right shoulder. As soon as he jumped into the passenger seat, Snake's black ass immediately began surveying the van's interior, especially all the advanced driving controls near the steering wheel. He started laughing.

"What's so damn funny?" I asked, annoyed by his ugly facial expressions. I'd never get used to him. I couldn't stand him.

Snake shook his head.

"Why are you shaking your head? And what's so fucking funny?"

"First, a pimped out wheelchair. Now, a rigged up caravan?"

"Fuck you, Snake."

"Just make sure you know how to drive this muthafucka. And make sure you stay at the speed limit and stop at all red lights. The last thing we need is for the cops to pull us over. Us getting searched means jail time for the both of us."

"I know, damn. I'm not a rookie."

"Look, I don't give a damn what you are. It's goin' to take more than a rigged up caravan to impress me. Rocco might be impressed with your ass, but I'm not. Real talk, I don't trust you."

I glared at him.

"Just make sure that when we get to the spot, you're on point. Rocco ain't here to keep me off your ass right now. It's *my* life that'll be on the line out there. So, if you even *look* like you're gonna fuck up out there at any moment, I will bury you." He leaned back into his seat. "Now, drive."

My only comeback was, "Whatever."

When I pulled away from the curb, we headed to the spot. Within fifteen minutes, we were in an alley behind an old ran down pawn shop. I stopped a good distance away from a white Tahoe.

Snake looked around, making sure there were no police or surprises. Satisfied, he said, "Alright, Ms. Special Needs, it's show time."

"My name is Keema, asshole."

Instead of being compassionate, he just laughed in my face. "Take the bag."

I was taken by surprise. He was supposed to make the transaction.

"What do you mean take the bag?" I questioned.

"I mean take the damn bag."

"Why?"

"Because you're gonna make the transaction."

"What? But I thought you were gonna do it. Do you know how stupid it's gonna look if I do it?"

"Well, Rocco should've thought about that before he put a handicap muthafucka on the payroll. Furthermore, do you think I'm slow? There's no way in hell I trust you to watch my back. How is a crippled bitch gonna be able to hold shit down if things go wrong?" he stated. "Nah, I'm not takin' that chance. *You're* gonna make the transaction and *I'll* hold *your* back."

"Snake, I don't like this."

"Bitch, do you think I give a fuck about what you like? This shit ain't up for discussion."

"Snake, this is serious. I can't be seen doing this. I'm still on papers."

He pulled out his gun, resting it on his side. "You should've thought about that before signin' up for the job. Now, if your ass don't make this transaction, shit gon' get even more serious. You gon' be a dead bitch. Shit don't get no more serious than that."

He tossed the bag in my lap, climbed out of the van and made his way to the back. Seconds later, he snatched the door open, then roughly picked me up and tossed me into the wheelchair.

"Damn, nigga," I fumed. "I ain't a damn rag doll."

"Whatever, just roll your ass over there and get this shit done. We ain't got all day."

Instead of arguing, I reluctantly did what I was told. Besides, going back and forth with his black ass wasn't gonna solve anything. It was obvious he had his mind made up.

Leaning against the hood of the van, he shouted, "And don't come back without the money! If you do, I'm gonna drive you to the nearest freeway and roll your ass out into oncomin' traffic!"

"Fuck you!" I shouted back.

I constantly looked around, wondering if anybody was watching me as I made my way towards the truck. Seconds later, I rolled up to the driver's door of the Tahoe. It's window came down slowly. A young dude with fuzzy, unkept corn rows sat in the driver's seat while a goofy looking white dude with bright red pimples on his cheeks sat in the passenger's seat. Both of them looked at me suspiciously.

"Who the fuck are you?" the driver asked.

"Keema."

"Is this shit a joke?"

"Does it look like a joke?"

"Where the hell is Snake or Rocco?" He looked in his rear view mirror nervously.

"They sent me."

He displayed a confused expression. "A bitch in a wheelchair."

"Yeah, a bitch in a wheelchair. And if you have a problem with that, I can leave."

"Look, no disrespect, but we don't know you and we don't like dealin' wit' new faces."

I shook my head and shrugged my shoulders like I could care less what his problem was.

He looked me up and down. It looked like he was about to pull off until he looked at the bag in my lap. He studied me for a few more seconds. "Is that the shit?"

"Yeah, you got the money?"

"Don't worry about all that. Just give me the bag."

"Look, I'm not giving you anything until…"

Instantly, both he and his friend pointed guns at me. My heart rate sped up at the sight of the two black Glock Dessert Eagles.

"The shit ain't up to be discussed, bitch. Give me the bag."

I handed the bag over, hoping they wouldn't kill me.

The dude in the driver's seat grabbed the bag, then handed it to his friend. At that point, the white guy opened the bag, cut one of the two kilos of heroin open and tasted it. Satisfied, he nodded to the driver. The driver then pulled a bag from beneath his seat and handed it to me.

"Good doin' business with you. Tell Rocco I said to hit me up if the plans change next time. That shit won't cool."

With that said, he turned up the SUV's stereo, rolled up his window and pulled off. Relieved, I exhaled a deep breath, but still needed a moment to pull myself together. Having a gun pointed at me instantly brought back memories of Frenchie ruining my life.

"Come on…we ain't got all day for you to daydream. We got shit to do!" Snake yelled.

Suddenly, my cell phone rang as I turned to head back to the van. Seeing that it was Toy, I wondered why Treasure's friend was calling me. I answered as I neared the van. With panic in her voice, she said something that made having guns pointed in my face pale in comparison. My mouth dropped as I stopped the wheelchair and just sat there in shock.

"Come on!" Snake shouted impatiently. "We gotta go!"

I couldn't hear him. I couldn't hear anything around me. All I could hear were the shocking words coming from Toy's mouth.

Chapter 15-

Treasure

I sat in the passenger seat of Rocco's car with my back leaned deeply into its soft butter leather. Rocco was in the driver's seat maneuvering through traffic with one hand and with no problem. His arm was still in a sling as we headed to the detail shop to finally get my car. Neither of us had been there since the shit jumped off with Vegas a week ago.

"What the nigga look like?" the voice of one of Rocco's homies came through the speaker of his cell phone which sat on the center console.

Rocco gave a description and began to give details regarding where Vegas could possibly be found, including Maya's address.

"I've got twenty stacks for any nigga who can lead me to him or bring me his muthafuckin' head," Rocco instructed.

Rocco was much more furious about what Vegas had done to me than what had been done to him. But he was handling it calmly. That was one of the reasons why I fell in love with him. He always played his hand close to his chest and never let his emotions dictate his decisions. He never let them show, at least not around me.

The interior of the car was filled with weed smoke as the two of us passed a blunt. Both of us needed to calm our nerves. Rocco himself was also taking an occasional sip from his bottle of Ciroc. There was no chaser. He drank it absolutely straight.

As Rocco conversed with his goon, I just sat there in silence seething in my yearning for vengeance. Of course I wanted Vegas myself. I couldn't wait to lay hands on him. When the moment came, I was gonna cut his fucking balls off and feed them to him. The only thing that overshadowed my want for vengeance was anger for what Toy's dumb ass had done. I couldn't believe that goofy bitch let Maya go. She hung up on me right after she'd given me the disturbing news. I'd been calling her ass ever since but got no answer. I'd been texting and even inboxed the bitch on Facebook, and direct messaged her on Twitter. She never responded.

The shit had me super worried. I had no idea where Maya was at this point or if she'd gone to the police. I was so worried about it that I hadn't slept a wink all night. Each time I tried, I would always have a nightmare about the cops kicking the hotel door in with their guns out and dragging my ass off to jail. The shit was terrifying. Obviously, the last place I wanted to see was a cramped ass cell. I had things to do. Sitting in jail around a bunch of dike looking broads wasn't gonna cut it for me. Plus, I like dick. No, change that. I absolutely *love, crave and need* dick. There's no way in hell I could go years without it. I know I couldn't.

I was also pissed off beyond understanding. By setting Maya free, Toy had fucked up the damn money. There was no way I'd be able to get the money from her cousin now. When I finally got my hands around her fucking neck, I was going to choke it until her eyes rolled to the back of her head.

Just like Rocco was now putting a bounty on Vegas' head, I was seriously thinking about putting one on Toy's. I wanted her just that badly. Fuck the history we had together. She'd fucked up too much damn money and I wasn't going to let her ass slide for this.

Rocco ended his call and glanced at me while still driving. He saw the concerned look on my face. "You alright?"

Shaking my head, I said, "Nah, Rocco, that bitch played me. I can't get over it."

"Look, Treasure, I know you upset, but you gotta let that shit go. It's probably for the best anyway because you should've never involved a child."

"I know, baby. But I just can't get it out of my head. I can't believe Toy would do some stupid shit like that."

"That's just the way shit happens sometimes. When you out here in these streets, you come across different breeds. Some are real, some fake. Once you've distinguished the two, you just gotta make adjustments and keep movin'."

He was dropping game and experience, but I truly wasn't listening. I wanted Toy to pay for what she did...badly.

"Let that shit go," he said while handing me the blunt. "At least for now, alright?"

I said, "Alright." But it was said with reluctance and done just to pacify him.

In all reality, I wasn't about to let what Toy did to me go, at all. She betrayed me and she fucked up my money. Those were cardinal sins in my damn book. I vowed right then and there as I took a huge pull of the blunt to get her back by any means necessary.

When Rocco stopped at a light, his new iPhone rang again. "What up?" he answered, placing the call on speaker once again.

As soon as he heard the person's voice, he immediately took the call off speaker and placed the phone between his shoulder and jaw. As he began to speak in several different codes, I knew exactly what the call was about.

"Alright," he said after a few moments. "I got you. Hit

Keema on her cell. I can't get at you right now. I got shit to handle, but Keema will get you straight."

Hearing him mention my mother's name elevated my anger. I hadn't spoken to that bitch since our fight the day before, and my spite for her was still fresh. Just like Toy, she'd played games with my damn money. She'd stolen from me. My own damn mother. That shit still had me furious.

Rocco's decision to hire her in the first place had me feeling some kind of way about him, too. It seemed kind of sick to me for him to hire a woman who couldn't even walk. Rocco told me that he'd hired her because of her experience in the game, but mainly because her confinement in the chair would throw the police off in certain situations.

As a runner for him, it would work out in both of their favors. He seemed to think that the police would never suspect a woman in a wheelchair of running drugs, and if they did, Keema had enough experience in the game to know how to handle herself. I'd even heard that she'd made a few moves for Rocco and came through with flying colors. But despite how much of a star player she was becoming, I still didn't trust her. My mother was a poisonous snake willing to bite anyone, including the hand that fed her.

Rocco finally pulled up at the detail shop. The sight of it made my stomach drop. Immediately, I remembered what had happened the last time I was here. My nostrils could once again, through imagination and memory, smell Vegas' flesh pressed against mine. My eyes could once again see his face. My anxiety went into overdrive.

Rocco grabbed his gun from beneath his seat and climbed out of the car. He didn't tuck the gun in his belt or make any attempts at concealing it. He held it firmly in his hand for anyone to see. Rocco wasn't sure if Vegas was possibly hiding somewhere watching and waiting to ambush him. But if that was the case, Rocco was prepared.

I watched, too. My eyes darted all over the street for any

signs of Vegas as I twisted and turned around in my seat several times. Fuck the mirrors. I didn't trust them. I wanted to see his ass with my naked eyes.

Rocco walked into the detail shop. As soon as he did, I locked the doors and continued to keep a careful look out for Vegas or anything suspicious. I didn't know exactly what I would do if something jumped off though. I didn't have a gun, so I'd most likely have to blow the shit out of the horn. When Rocco finally came out of the shop, a short, Spanish guy stood beside him. He signaled for me to get out of the car. As I stepped out, another Spanish guy pulled my car from behind the shop and stopped at the end of the alley.

Rocco handed me the keys. "Take the car and go home."

"But I want to stay with you," I told him with disappointment.

"We'll hook up later on. I gotta handle some things and I don't want you with me just in case shit jumps off."

I was still disappointed and it showed on my face. If something did happen, I wanted to be with him. Seeing the look on my face, Rocco gave me a soft peck on my lips.

"Everything's gonna be alright. We'll hook up later. I promise."

Finally, I agreed and headed to the car.

"Go straight home," he instructed. "Real talk…until we get this shit with Vegas resolved, I don't want you out here in these streets."

"I got you," I said, knowing I was lying. Fuck going home. I was about to get out in these streets and find Toy's monkey ass.

After climbing into the car, I immediately turned the radio to 92.3 and bobbed my head as ASAP Rocky's song, *Fuckin' Problems* blasted through the speakers. It felt good to be back in my own car. All I needed now was another blunt to really set shit off. As I pulled out of the alley and approached the corner, a text came through my cell.

Got your money!! All sixty grand!

The text was from Kendrick. I smiled. That was the best news I'd heard in a minute. Shit, with everything that had been going on lately, I'd honestly forgotten about Kendrick. It was on now though. I immediately texted him back.

Good. Glad ur pedophile ass decided to cooperate. Meet me at Eastpoint Mall tomorrow at eleven a.m. Don't be late.

After sliding the phone back into my purse, moments later I pulled up at Toy's apartment complex and jumped out of the car. I wasn't sure what I was going to do with her if she answered the door. At the moment, I'd probably let her ride; let her think things were good between us. What I wanted at the moment was to just see her face and talk her into trusting me. Then I'd know where she was when I finally decided to settle the score.

As I made my way towards the building, my phone rang. Taking it from my purse, I saw a number on the screen that I didn't recognize. Usually I didn't answer numbers that I didn't know, but for some reason I decided to answer this one.

"Can I speak to Maya?" the voice on the other end asked.

The question made me stop dead in my tracks. Why was this woman calling my phone and asking for Maya. Another strange thing about the call was that the voice sounded familiar. I couldn't place it, but I'd definitely heard it before.

"Who's this?"

"This is her cousin. She called me from this number a few days ago. I've been trying to reach her since I got into town, but she's not answering her phone. I'm kind of worried."

Instincts and reflexes jumped in. I thought about the money. Here was my chance to possibly still get it.

"Maya told me she was in a bind when we last spoke and she really needed me to bring her something. I haven't been able to reach her since. Her husband and I are worried to death," the woman continued.

Her husband, I thought.

Those two words sent electric bolts through my body. "Her husband?" I asked.

"Yeah, he's worried about her and their son."

The bitch knew where Vegas was. She could serve his ass to me on a silver platter and didn't even know it. My eyes lit up like stars.

"I think I know where she is," I said, lying.

"Where?" she asked excitedly.

"Hold up a second. It's going to cost you."

"Cost me? What do you mean? Look, this isn't a game. I need to know where my cousin is."

"And, I'll tell you. But you have to understand that I have needs. I haven't gotten high in days and my body is starting to go into withdrawal. I need a hit bad."

"Look, whatever, just tell me where Maya is and I'll make sure you can buy enough damn crack to smoke yourself into a coma."

With a smile, I gave her an address and told her to meet me there in one hour. As soon as our conversation was done, I instantly called Rocco.

"What's up, baby?" he answered.

"Guess what."

"What?"

"I found Vegas."

He paused for a second, obviously in shock. "Yo', are you serious?"

"Yeah, so I need you to meet me."

I gave him the address to where I'd planned to meet Maya's cousin and told him to meet me there, too. After hanging up, I dashed back to my car, hopped in and sped away from the curb headed to the meeting spot. I arrived in the parking lot of the skating rink on Pennsylvania Avenue in no time. After parking between two cars, I shut off the engine and watched the lot's entrance so I'd be able to see Maya's cousin when she pulled up. I wanted to be there super early so I'd be able to see anything strange.

As I sat there in silence, thoughts invaded my mind from all directions. Revenge was so near. Money was also near. I'd be able to get both just like I'd planned when I had Maya's ass begging for her life. I wasn't gonna be able to get the amount I originally asked for, but something was better than nothing. I couldn't wait. But along with those thoughts, another thought surfaced, one that threw a little shade my way...

Why hadn't Maya called her cousin yet?

That didn't make sense. If Maya was now free, why hadn't she called her cousin to tell her she was okay? Why hadn't she answered her phone? That didn't make sense. Something wasn't right. Before I could dwell on it too long, I saw a new, pearl white Range Rover stop in the skating rink's parking lot. Its windows weren't tinted so I was able to see two men and a woman sitting inside. They were all studying the parking lot. I wondered if the woman was Maya's cousin. If it was, one of the men was possibly Vegas. I couldn't tell because the car was too far away. Moments later, the passenger's side door finally opened, and Vegas stepped out. The sight of him made me lean forward in my seat. Immediately, I grabbed my phone to call Rocco and let him know Vegas was definitely here. As the phone rang, I continued to watch the car as the driver's door opened. My eyes were locked on it as a woman stepped out. When I saw her face, the blood in my head plunged to my feet. My face twisted in disbelief.

The woman was Shy!

"What the fuck?" I said to myself in disbelief, while still holding the phone to my ear.

At that moment, the passenger's back door opened and the second man stepped out.

"I'm on my way, baby," Rocco said finally answering the phone.

He got no response from me.

"Treasure, you there? Did you hear me?"

He still got no response.

"Treasure?"

I couldn't utter a single, solitary syllable. My mouth was wide open, but no words fell out. None could be manufactured. I was too far in shock to speak.

"Treasure?"

The phone fell from my hand and dropped in my lap. My eyes stared at the man who'd climbed out of the car without blinking. At the moment, nothing else mattered. No one else existed. No other sounds could be heard. The only thing that mattered at that moment was that I was staring at the man who'd put my mother in a wheelchair...

FRENCHIE!

Chapter 16-
Treasure

I was totally frozen and speechless. It was like I was staring at the devil himself. The sight of him wouldn't allow my body to physically react. It was as if I was caught in some kind of trance. Before that moment, I'd never seen anything or anyone who made me react that way. It was the craziest feeling, completely indescribable.

Inside, I didn't know whether to panic or to hit the push button start of my car and get the fuck outta dodge. Completely unprepared and caught off guard, I didn't know how to react. But after contemplating a few seconds, I realized staying put would be my best option. If I started my car and pulled out, it would possibly draw unwanted attention. Even though my windows were tinted, I didn't want to chance anyone seeing me, especially since Vegas had seen my car at the detail shop.

Frenchie was dressed in a grey sweat suit with a big ass obnoxious Polo symbol on the side. His head was now shaved bald, and from what I remembered, he'd definitely gained weight. His beard was freshly trimmed but thick, similar to

Suge Knight. A thick platinum chain with a gorgeous Jesus piece hung around his neck, while both of his ear lobes rocked huge brilliant diamonds. Shy was just fashionable. Wearing a pair of super tight skinny jeans that hugged her hips and thighs perfectly, she also rocked a pair of six-inch platform red bottoms that gave her calves crazy definition. She'd even stepped her weave game up.

I'd heard Frenchie was always into getting money. Evidently, none of that had changed. There was no doubt in my mind that he'd flipped the money he shot my mother over. By now, he'd probably flipped it enough times to turn it into several hundred thousand or even a million. That's just how seasoned a hustler he was.

I slid down into my seat; not wanting anyone to see me. I still had no idea exactly what to do. My mind drifted back to that day four years ago. I could still clearly see the gun in Frenchie's hand as he stood over my mother. My ears could still hear Shy urging him to kill her. It was as if it had just happened yesterday or even five minutes ago. That's just how fresh the memory was in my head. I'd never forget it. But above all, I'd never forget hearing the gun go off, seeing the blaze from its barrel and watching the bullets viciously tear into my mother. I'd seen a lot up until that point. But that moment shook me. It had been the second time I had seen my mother shot.

"Treasure!" Rocco's voice came through my phone, finally waking me up from a deep daze.

I grabbed the phone from my lap. "Baby," I said rapidly. "I need you to get here as soon as possible." My eyes were still locked directly on Frechie, Shy and Vegas.

"Yo', what's up? I been callin' yo' name for a minute. You a'ight?"

"For now, but I don't know how long that's gonna last. I need you to get here quick."

"I'm comin'. I'm about five minutes away."

I told Rocco exactly where my car was, then told him to

park behind me when he got there.

"Bet," he said and hung up.

Sitting the phone down, I continued to watch the movements of all three of them like a hawk. Moments later, Frenchie said something to Shy that I couldn't make out. She nodded, reached into the pocket of her jeans and pulled out a cell phone. She then dialed a number and placed the phone to her ear. A second later my phone rang. Looking down at the same unknown number, who would've ever thought that Shy would end up being Maya's cousin? It was a crazy fucking coincidence. Not knowing what to say yet, instead of answering, I let the phone ring.

Within minutes, I suddenly saw Rocco pull into the lot. My anxiety subsided, but not by much. Just like I'd told him, Rocco pulled behind my car, then got out with his boy, Snake following closely behind. Snake was no doubt strapped up, loyally keeping an eye on his boss and ready to put a hole in anything moving. They jumped into my car.

"Did you see him?" I asked Rocco as soon as he was in the passenger seat.

"Nah, where he at?"

I pointed across the street and looked at Rocco. I could see the muscles in his jaw clench. I could also see his lips curl into something close to a sneer. Vegas had violated him. The memory of it all was probably playing itself inside his head at the moment. I could see it.

"I can't wait to smoke that nigga. On everything I love, I can't wait," he said with spite in his voice.

"You want me to go over there and blaze that nigga right now?" Snake asked. "You know I got that heat on me."

"Nah, hold up. Who's them muthafuckas with him?" Rocco looked at me.

I watched Frenchie and Shy through the windshield.

Rocco looked at me. "Treasure, who them two muthafuckas with him?"

I could feel Snake staring at the back of my head.

"The people who put my mother in a wheelchair," I finally answered.

Rocco looked at me strangely. "What?"

"Damn," Snake said. "Maybe instead of shootin' them, we should go over there and shake their hands."

I turned around and gave him a look of death. "Fuck you, Snake."

"No disrespect, Treasure but you know your mom is a grimy bitch. I see it in her. Shit, if she ever crosses me, fuck puttin' her in a wheel hair. I'm gonna put that bitch in a *cemetery* and call it a day," Snake added.

With his eyes locked on me, Rocco asked, "So, what did your mother do?"

Immediately, my mind drifted back to that dreadful day on the sidewalk. I could still feel and smell the blood leaking from my mother's body. I could still see her losing consciousness. I could still see myself, Deniro, Shane and even Ms. Kyle crying over her as Frenchie and Shy dashed to their car and sped off.

"Yeah, what did she do?" Snake questioned. "I bet it was some super foul shit, wasn't it? She looks like the type who'd sell her own mother out for a few dollars."

If he only knew how correct he was, I thought to myself. Both sets of eyes were on me.

"It's a long story," I finally said, not ready to tell it. "Just know, Rocco, that I told you I didn't agree with you hiring her to work for you."

My phone rang again. Staring across the street, I saw Shy on her phone again. Without having to look at the screen, I knew it was her calling. This time I answered.

"Hey, where are you?" Shy asked.

"Oh, my God. I was in a car accident! Somebody ran a red light and rammed straight into my car. My leg...my leg hurts really bad." As I tried to make my voice sound shaky, I could see Frenchie and Vegas looking at Shy with curious eyes.

"Are you serious? Well, are you hurt? Are you still gonna be able to come here?" Shy asked. "I hate to be insensitive, but I really need to know where my cousin is."

"I'm gonna have to call you back. I'm on my way to the hospital."

"But…"

"I'm gonna have to call you back."

After hanging up, I watched Shy tell Frenchie and Vegas something. They huddled for a moment, then eventually got back in the truck.

"Where are they going?" Rocco questioned.

"I don't know," I told him.

Quickly Rocco said, "Yo' Snake, go hop in my car. We're gonna follow these muthafuckas." He tossed Snake his keys.

"Bet," Snake replied, then got out.

With those words said, Rocco promptly hopped out of the passenger's seat and dashed around to the driver's side of my car. He obviously thought that he was a faster driver. Rocco then told me to move over. Seconds later, we pulled out of the lot and began to follow the Range Rover. Even though we stayed a few cars behind, I still noticed the Delaware plates.

They must've moved there after the shooting, I thought.

"Treasure, I need some answers," Rocco suddenly blurted out.

"About what?"

"Everything. I've got a nigga I've never met before shootin' at me. I'm in a shootout with some old nigga who tried to set me up. Now, I'm followin' some people who put your mom in a wheelchair. I need answers."

Damn, I couldn't deny the fact that everything bad that had been happening to him lately revolved around me. He deserved answers. Usually, I wouldn't have entertained the thought of telling a nigga anything about how I truly get down.

But Rocco wasn't just *any* nigga. He was my heart.

I sighed before telling Rocco everything about my scam. I told him every detail including how I usually picked the dudes, to how much money I'd made over the past year. I even told him all about Vegas, and that it was me who was responsible for getting him shot. I ended with the short version of how and why my mother ended up disabled. Although I was nervous, in the end the shit was like therapy. It felt good to finally get everything out in the open.

"Baby, I should've told you everything in the beginning, but I just couldn't. Besides, I didn't feel the need to be honest because at first I thought you were just gonna be another dude that I fucked with. But now I'm checking for you, so I feel bad that I wasn't truthful. I didn't know I was gonna fall in love with you. I'm sorry I had to be so secretive."

He looked at me like I was crazy. "You're *sorry* for being so secretive," he stated angrily. You're *sorry*?"

My body tensed up.

"Being secretive almost got me killed, Treasure!"

"Baby, I know, and I'm sorry. From now on I'll be up front about everything. I promise."

"That doesn't change things, Treasure. Shit is in motion now. Blood has been spilled and even more is about to spill."

My eyes fell sadly to my lap.

"That secretive shit is why we're here right now!"

I felt like a child being scolded.

"Well, Rocco, it's not like I'm the only secretive one in this relationship. You're secretive, too. You talk in codes every time you get a call, and you never talk about your family."

"Because you don't need to know *everything* about my business or my family. If the cops bust me, the less you know, the less you can tell."

"I'd never tell on you."

"Yeah, that sounds good. But when those white muthafuckas got your ass in one of those back rooms; tellin' you you lookin' at a hundred years, it might loosen your tongue a little bit."

"Rocco, I'm not like those other bitches. I'm loyal," I replied with a insulted tone.

"You sure about that?"

"Hell yeah, I'm sure."

With that said, the car fell silent. Neither of us said anything else as we continued to follow the Range. I wasn't sure what he was thinking. All I could do was hope it wasn't something terrible. I loved him and didn't want to lose him.

Finally, the Range pulled into the parking lot of the Aloft hotel in Arundel Mills. It didn't even surprise me that they were staying so far out. Guess the less they were seen in the city…the better. We pulled into the lot also and parked at a safe distance away from them. Snake pulled into the lot with Rocco's car seconds later and parked near us. We watched as Frenchie, Shy and Vegas got out of the truck. As Vegas gave Frenchie some dap and hugged Shy, my eyes zoomed directly in on a Louis Vuitton duffle bag that hung from Frenchie's shoulder. I wasn't sure if it contained the money that Maya had requested or not, but I needed to find out if it did.

Within seconds, Vegas headed across the parking lot to his Audi A8 while Frenchie and Shy made their way towards the entrance of the hotel. When Vegas started his car and headed for the lot's exit, Rocco quickly got on his cell and called Snake.

"Yo', Snake. Stay here and watch them muthafuckas in the Range. We're goin' after that nigga, Vegas. If they roll out, follow them," Rocco instructed.

Anticipation had a humongous hold on me as I stared out of the window. The shit was overwhelming and my nerves were in overdrive. We seemed to be driving forever and I had no idea where we were headed, especially when we passed a

Washington, D.C. sign. When Vegas finally got off the highway, he made several turns, then began to slow down when he approached a construction site. Silently, we both wondered what was going on when he stopped the car, especially when a man in a dark hoodie and Timberland boots rapidly approached the car and jumped inside. Vegas once again pulled off. At that moment, we had no idea what to expect. Was it a drug deal? Did Vegas realize that we were following him and went to get back up? Neither of us had any idea. We just continued to follow them.

After a few more turns, Vegas' car came to another stop, this time on a dead end street that was surrounded by woods. Rocco made sure to pull over where they wouldn't notice us as we continued to watch. From a safe distance we could see, but only the back of their heads. Suddenly, the two heads did something that shocked both me and Rocco...

They connected, appearing to be kissing.

"What the fuck?" Rocco said surprised.

My mouth dropped.

Both of us were taken completely by surprise.

We were even more surprised when the head of the man who'd hopped into the car dropped down and out of sight. It was obvious he was giving Vegas some head.

"Wowwwwwww," was all I could say.

"Aye, I'm not about to watch this sick shit," Rocco said in disgust as he pulled a gun from underneath the seat, jumped out of the car and made his way towards the two men.

He obviously recognized this as the perfect chance for get back.

"Wait for me," I said, getting out of the car, too.

I didn't want to miss a second of what was about to go down. When we snuck up to the car and looked in the window, Vegas' head was lying back on the headrest. His eyes were closed and the palm of his right hand was on the back of the other man's head; guiding it up and down. Shaking his head,

Rocco tapped the barrel of the gun against the window causing Vegas' eyes to quickly open. When he realized who it was, they opened even wider.

"Get yo' faggot ass out the car, nigga!" Rocco demanded.

I guess Vegas decided not to make it a debate as he did exactly what he was told. He didn't even have time to put his dick back in his pants. The other man, obviously scared, reached for the handle of the passenger door.

"Nah, nigga," Rocco told him. "Stay yo' dick suckin' ass in there and keep yo' hands where I can see 'em. And if you make one fuckin' move, I'ma blast yo' bitch ass."

The man placed his hands where they could be seen and sat still.

Rocco turned his attention back to Vegas. "So, you one of them down low muthafuckas, huh?"

"I knew I should'a made sure you were dead," Vegas responded.

"Yeah, yo' mistake. Now, that mistake is gonna cost you," Rocco fired back.

"Where's my money, Vegas?" I yelled at him.

Vegas looked at me. "Fuck you, bitch," he spat. "I ain't payin' you shit."

"You trifling muthafucka," I spewed. "Is this faggot nigga the reason why you didn't come to see about your own wife and son the other night?"

Vegas' entire expression changed. He looked at me suspiciously. "So, you were there the night my wife called and said somethin' was wrong with my son? You were there the night they went missing?"

"Yup."

"So, where are they?"

"Fuck you. If you ain't paying...I ain't saying," I replied.

Like a deranged animal, he charged at me. "You treacherous, bitch! Where is my family? Where is my family?"

Before I could react, Vegas knocked me to the ground and was on top of me with his hands wrapped around my neck.

"Where's my family?" he screamed again.

Blood sprayed into my face as soon as the gun went off. Vegas' body collapsed on top of me.

Then everything went silent.

Rocco had shot Vegas in the back of the head. He was dead before his body fell against mine. Realizing it, all I could do was lay there in shock. The moment was surreal.

Suddenly, the passenger door of Vegas' car opened. The other man hopped out and took off running. With no hesitation, Rocco rapidly made his way around the back of the car, took aim and pulled the trigger. The bullet from his gun tore right into the center of the fleeing man's back. He dropped to the ground immediately. Rocco then ran up on him and shot him in the back of the head to ensure he was dead.

Still, with blood all over my face and even in my mouth, all I could do was lay underneath Vegas' dead body unable to move, unable to speak or scream. All I could do was wonder how I had allowed myself to become the woman I'd despised my mother so much for being.

Chapter 17-

Keema

My fingers held the joystick on the armrest of my wheelchair tightly. As the wheels rolled up the sidewalk and into the overgrown grass, all I could do was worry. From the way Toy sounded over the phone, it was obvious something was wrong. I just wasn't exactly sure what it was. Toy wouldn't tell me, but there was definitely panic in her voice. I didn't want to imagine the possibilities, but I had no choice. All I could do was hope it wasn't too bad, and that Treasure wasn't hurt. Although I wasn't feeling my daughter at the moment, I still didn't want anything life threatening to happen to her.

After rolling up to the door on the side of the house, I knocked three times like Toy requested. Anxiously, I waited for her to answer while looking back to make sure no one was watching me. Obviously, a wheelchair bound woman rolling up to the door of a boarded up, vacant house would draw suspicion. I had a bad feeling that whatever Toy was involved in, I wasn't gonna like it.

After not getting an answer, I knocked again. Damn, I hoped shit wasn't as bad as it seemed. I couldn't afford any trouble right now. After several seconds, I finally heard foot-steps approaching from the other side. A moment later, it opened.

"What took you so long?" Toy asked. She looked terrible.

"What the fuck do you mean, what took me so long? I gotta job now, so I came as soon as I could."

"Hurry up and get in here."

"Look, stop giving me orders. *You* called *me* over here, remember?" I looked at the small step by the door. "Did your dumb ass forget that I was in a wheelchair? How the hell am I supposed to get in there?" Luckily, the house was one level.

I wasn't exactly sure where the strength came from, but Toy managed to lift my chair, one side at a time until she maneuvered me inside. She then peeked outside and looked around to make sure no one had followed me. Satisfied, she closed the door.

"So, what's going on?" I asked. "What's so important? And why do you look like that?" I gazed at her wild hair and puffy, swollen eyes. It looked like she'd been crying for hours.

Instead of answering, Toy started pacing the floor and wringing out her hands like wash cloths. Her nerves seemed completely shot.

"Toy, what happened?"

"Keema, I didn't mean it. I swear to God I didn't mean it."

"Mean what, Toy. What happened?"

"I can't believe this shit," she said, continuing to pace nervously. "I killed her. Oh God, I killed her."

The words hit me hard.

"Killed who? What are you talking about?" I prayed to God she wasn't talking about Treasure.

"I don't know what to do, Keema. What am I gonna do?"

"Toy, who did you kill? Talk to me."

Still, I couldn't get an understandable answer, just nervous and panic filled mumbling.

Suddenly, I heard what appeared to be crying coming from another room.

I frowned. "Who the hell is that?"

Toy still didn't respond.

Realizing that I had to find out shit on my own, I made my way towards the living room. I knew then I definitely wasn't going to like what I was about to see. Something told me to stop, turn around and leave Toy on her own; that whatever was going on was her business and not mine. Something told me that whatever I was getting ready to roll up on was going to throw a monkey wrench in my own shit. Sure enough, I was right. Lying on the floor was a woman. Her eyes were lifeless and staring directly up at the ceiling while the back of her head, or at least what was left of it, was lying in a pool of blood and brain fragments. A little boy sat beside her crying.

"What the fuck?" I gasped, stopping as soon as I saw the dead body.

Toy walked into the living room holding her head. "What are we going to do?"

"What did you do?"

"I didn't mean it. I swear I didn't."

"What you didn't mean to do is pointless now because she's dead."

"Are you sure she's dead?" Toy asked dumbfounded.

I looked at the goofy bitch like she'd lost her mind. "What the fuck do you mean *is she dead*?"

"I…I…I mean maybe she just needs mouth to mouth or somethin'. Maybe she's just in shock."

Toy stopped pacing for a moment and looked at me like she hoped I could perform a miracle, hoping I could do magic.

"Mouth to mouth?" I stared at her. This bitch was obviously delirious. "Are you serious right now?"

Toy grabbed her head and began to pace again.

"What happened?"

"It wasn't on purpose…it wasn't. I didn't mean to kill Maya."

"Well, how did it happen?"

"She…she went for the gun and it went…went off," Toy stuttered.

"What the hell were y'all doing up in a vacant house in the first place?"

"It was the best place I knew to hide her and the kid."

"What are you talking about, Toy? What were you hiding them for? Is that his mother?"

She nodded her head. "I was hidin' them because it was the only way me and Treasure could get the money."

The mention of Treasure's name turned my attention on like a light bulb. Quickly, Toy began to tell me about her and Treasure's plan. Everything seemed to be working out for them until for whatever reason, Treasure stopped answering her phone. Toy assumed Treasure had gotten the money from Maya's cousin somehow and was going to keep it while leaving Toy hanging out to dry. Somehow shortly after, Maya and Toy got into a struggle over the gun and it went off, killing Maya. Now, Toy was totally lost. She had no idea what to do.

"Keema, that's why I called you. I didn't know who else to call. I don't know what else to do. I'm scared to death."

I shook my head. "Damn young girls. Y'all bitches love to act all hard; like y'all know what to do out in these streets. When in actuality, y'all don't know shit."

"Well, what are we gonna do?"

"*We?*" I asked, wondering how the fuck it became *we* all of a sudden. "*We* didn't kidnap that woman and her child. *We* didn't blow her brains all over the floor. *You* did that shit, Toy."

"I know, but now I need help, Keema. Please help me out," she begged.

Seeing the little boy crying over his dead mother's body had me clueless. Now, I really regretted coming over here. If the cops found out about this, my name would possibly be involved. Toy was the type of scary bitch who would put me in it. I could see it in her. I was still on probation. I couldn't be involved with some shit like this.

"Keema, what are we gonna do?" she asked me again.

Here she goes with that damn 'we' shit again, I thought.

"I don't know."

"What do you mean, you don't know?"

"I mean…I don't…fucking…know."

"Well, think of somethin'."

This bitch had a lot of nerve. "Why should I? *You* were the braniac who did this shit…not me."

"It was a mistake, okay? A damn mistake."

"Toy, a mistake is when you spill juice on the fucking carpet. This shit right here is life in prison, or death row!"

Toy looked like she was going to cry. "Keema, please help me. I don't wanna go to jail. I act tough, but I'm not really that way. They'll rape me in there."

She looked super pitiful.

"I don't know why I let Treasure talk me into this shit," she continued. "She's always short changin' me."

Damn, I felt bad for her. But despite my feelings, I thought about my situation. I was slowly but surely on a come up in Rocco's crew. I was earning his trust. The only thing that could possibly throw a monkey wrench in it was Treasure. I wanted her man, but obviously she wasn't going to give him up without a fight. That's when it dawned on me that I might be able to somehow use Toy and this situation to my advantage. Maybe Toy and I could pen the murder on Treasure. With Treasure away in prison, nothing would stop me from becoming Rocco's queen. Shit, me and him could be the next Jay-Z and Beyoncé. No, fuck that…we could be the next Barack and Michelle. Suddenly, the sobs of the crying little boy awoke me from dreams of such an ambitious future.

"Treasure, doesn't know you killed this woman, right?"

Toy nodded her head. "She just thinks I let her go."

Yeah, we could definitely spin this to work in my advantage, I thought to myself.

"Well, in that case, get the boy and let's go," I instructed.

"Why?"

"Just do it."

"But he saw everything. He knows my face. He can tell the cops," Toy whined.

"Will you just get him and come on?"

"But Keema, I'm not feelin' that. We should kill him. He's the only loose end."

Her and that damn *we* shit was getting on my nerves.

"Look, Toy, just do what I said."

"Well, what are we gonna do with him?"

"We're gonna bring him with us. We'll figure the rest out later. Come on."

She was still skeptical.

"Look, you want revenge on Treasure for playing you, right?"

Toy paused for a second. "Yeah."

"Well, this is the only way you're gonna get it. Now, grab him and come on." I wheeled toward the door.

When Toy finally grabbed the little boy and tried to follow me, I guess his little ass had other plans.

"Mommy!" the boy screamed as he kicked and clawed at Toy's arms. "Mommy!"

"Shut his ass up," I ordered.

Toy covered his mouth with her hand, but he still continued to kick and fight. It took us a few minutes to finally get out of the house between me needing help with the chair and that little bastard screaming to the top of his lungs, but somehow we managed. Moments later, we were in my van and headed down the street when my phone rang. Recognizing the Virginia area code, I answered.

"Yeah."

"Hey, Keema. How are you?"

"I'm a little busy right now, Ms. Kyle."

"Oh, well, I'll make it really quick. Deniro wants to come spend a few days with you. Oh, and thanks for the money by the way. It came in handy."

Damn, that wouldn't be a good idea right now. I had too much going on.

"I really think he needs this visit. He keeps having crying spells and nightmares. I don't know why. All I can say is that Deniro says he keeps seeing someone stabbing you in his dreams. He's worried to death about you," she included.

Obviously, I hated to hear that. I never wanted my baby to worry about me, but I just had far too much going on right now.

"Keema…"

Before she could say anything else, and instead of having the heart to tell her no, I said, "Ms. Kyle, I'm real busy right now. I'll call you right back."

"But…"

I hit the end button. I felt bad and guilty, but right now, Deniro would hold me up. He'd complicate things a little more than they already were. He was better off in Virginia right now.

Moments later, Toy's phone rang. She pulled it from her pocket and looked down at the screen. Before she placed it to her ear, I was able to see Rasheeda's name on the screen. As they talked, I ear hustled, but wasn't quite able to understand what was being said. They weren't quite talking in codes, but something about it still made me inquisitive.

As she continued to talk, a text came through my phone. While keeping an eye on the road, I grabbed my phone and read the message. It was from Shane asking me to come home. That nigga had never said that before. I hoped he wasn't whipped. I'd created a monster. All I could do was hope it wouldn't come back to haunt me.

Chapter 18-

Lil Kim's classic song, *Mafia's Land* from her head banging album, *Hardcore* thumped loudly from the speakers of my Benz's high-end sound system. I could remember my mother playing that CD all of the time, relating to the way Kim went about grinding and getting money. Now, I guess her choice in music had rubbed off on me. I loved that Kim and Foxy shit even more than Nicki Minaj. It always got me in the mood to get out here and get what I felt was owed to me. This moment was no different at all. Kim's lyrics were my mood music.

Reciting Kim's lyrics word for word, I was excited as the rims of my whip spun like windmills as I passed one street corner after the next. I'd just gotten my baby washed. The sun was shining so brightly, the beams falling from the cloudless morning sky had the black paint and chrome glimmering like new money.

It was moments like this that made me love being me. From bus stops, people gawked at me. I saw them whispering. I saw their stares. Clearly, some wanted to be me, while others hated me. Either way, my heart was content. Either way, I was a queen bitch and I was on their minds. But above all, while they were on their way to punch a clock at their low paying lame ass jobs, I was on my way to do what the fuck I do best…

GET MONEY!

I was allergic to being broke.

In twenty minutes, I would be pulling into the mall's parking lot to meet Kendrick and pick up the money he owed me. The shit had my pussy wet. Real talk; no exaggeration. Each time I thought about money, my panties would be drenched. Besides good dick, money was the only other thing in life that had that type of effect on me. I couldn't help it. I was addicted to sex and money.

Speaking of money, the duffle bag that Frenchie carried into the hotel had me curious. I had a feeling there was some-thing super important in it, most likely crisp hard cash. What-ever it was, I needed to get my hands on it.

The thought of calling my mother and letting her know that her nemesis was in town had crossed my mind. I wondered heavily if I should. Of course she would want to know. Of course she'd been wanting revenge ever since they left her ass to die. I should've called her immediately. A part of me wanted to, but another side of me dismissed it.

Me and my mother had a love/hate relationship. I didn't know which one I felt most. But I *did* know the bitch still had me super heated about stealing from me. That was something I couldn't quite get over. She had me so pissed that if Rocco wouldn't have pulled me off of her that day, I would've proba-bly killed her. It was a hell of an intention to have towards your own mother, but I couldn't help it. My mother was a devious bitch. She'd been that way for as long as I could remember. Fuck, her selfishness had cost my grandmother, and my baby brother their lives. That was something I'd never forgive her for, and something that would always complicate our bond.

Fuck it, I thought to myself.

Eventually, I'd tell my mother about Frenchie and Shy. For now though, it was all about my money. Frenchie and Shy were *her* enemies, not mine. If anything, I'd much rather rob them muthafuckas for that duffle bag and let *her* worry about everything else. Why should I take a chance on getting blood on my hands? Why the fuck should I worry? I had other matters to tend to.

Suddenly, Snake crossed my mind. He was supposed to be sitting outside the hotel at that very moment watching Frenchie's and Shy's every move. And like I said, I truly was interested in that duffle bag. I hadn't told Rocco my intentions yet, but I needed to know where that bag was at all times. I called Snake.

"What up?" he answered lazily on just the second ring. He sounded tired.

"Any movement?" I asked.

"Did I call you to tell you there was any fuckin' movement? Shit, when the fuck did it become a part of my job requirement to call you about a muthafuckin' thing? You don't pay me."

I was caught off guard by his response. "Hold up, nigga. Who do you think you're talking to?"

"I'm talkin' to your ass."

"Nah, nigga, you can't be."

"Why the fuck not? Since when do I take orders from you?"

"Fall back, Snake."

"Fuck that! Don't get shit twisted. You don't run shit around here. Just because you fuckin' the boss man doesn't mean you run shit."

"I didn't say I run shit."

"It ain't about what you *say*. It's about how you carry yourself. Just callin' to question me about some shit is the perfect example. Don't question me about nothin'."

"Snake…"

"Snake, my ass. I been out here all fuckin' night over some shit that you and your momma are involved in. I don't even know why. All I know is I'm hungry, I'm out of weed and I'm ready to go home and get up in some damn pussy. Now, if you want some info, let *that* be enough for you."

I'd had enough of his rants.

"Look, nigga, I don't know who you think you're talking to, but you better check yourself. I may not run shit, but if I tell Rocco that you're talking to me this way, you and I both know shit will get real ugly."

"Bitch, I'm his right hand man. I been puttin' in work since your ass was in diapers. Do you actually think he'll turn on me for *you*?"

"If I embellish shit, he will."

"So, you threatenin' to lie on me?"

"Let's just say I'm *not* a bitch you wanna piss off. I can make things out here very uncomfortable for you."

"What does that shit mean?"

"Fuck with me and find out."

Snake grew quiet. I didn't quite know whether to take his silence as him bowing down or as him silently plotting. I knew I was playing a dangerous game at the moment. Snake was a stone cold killer. Niggas like him didn't take threats lightly. But at same time, I knew being Rocco's girl meant I was stamped with a "HANDS OFF" policy. No matter how angry Snake was right now, as long as I was Rocco's girl, there was nothing he could do about it.

"I don't care how long you've been sitting out in front of that hotel and I don't care how much longer you've gotta be there," I told him. "Just do it. And when I call for an update, it would be in your best interest to answer the phone."

With that said, I hung up, knowing I'd gotten my point across. Still seething from having to check Snake's ass, I called Shy. Until I could come up with a good plan to get that damn bag, I would have to buy some time and do what I could to keep her from growing too suspicious.

Shy answered on the very first ring. "Hello."

"Hey, I'm sorry that I'm just calling you back, but I got pretty banged up in the accident," I lied. "I'm still in the hospital. Broke my leg in two different places and shattered my knee."

Evidently not interested in my well-being she said, "Look, I'm sorry about your accident and all, but I need to know where Maya is. This has gone on long enough."

Thinking quickly, I responded, "Alright, I'm gonna be honest with you."

"Haven't you been honest already?"

"I couldn't because Maya told me not to tell anyone."

"What do you mean? What's going on?"

"Things have been going on. I can't tell you exactly what they are. All I can say is her safety was threatened. People were after her."

"What people?"

"Just people. That's all I can say about it. She's hiding out right now and doesn't want anyone to know where she is until she can figure some things out."

"What about her son? Where is he?" Shy questioned.

"He's with her. He's fine."

"Well, does she have a number? We're worried sick. We really need to talk to them."

"I can't give it to you."

"Goddamn it!" she screamed angrily into the phone, losing her patience. "That's my fucking family. Give me the damn number!"

"I can't."

"Why not?"

"Because…" I paused to give what I was about to say some mystery and drama.

"Because what?"

I remained quiet, liking the building effect.

"Hello? Because what?"

Finally I said, "Because Vegas is the person she's running from."

This time Shy paused for a second. "What?"

"Yeah, I know it's a surprise. It was a surprise to me, too. I thought he was a nice guy."

"He is a nice guy," she defended.

"Well, I disagree. When a man has been beating your ass on a daily basis, I wouldn't consider him nice."

"Are you serious?"

"On everything I love. That's why I can't tell you where she is. You might lead Vegas right to her."

"Are you crazy? That's my cousin. Why would I lead that sorry ass nigga to her?"

"I'm just saying. Maya doesn't want to take any chances. Vegas tried to kill her the last time."

"Look, she needs to be around family right now. Tell me where she is so I can come get her."

"I can't."

"Look, whoever the fuck you are. Tell me or I'm calling the damn cops!"

"Do what you feel you have to do. But just know, I'm not talking to any damn police. You're lucky I'm even talking to *you*. I don't want to be involved. I've got enough problems of my own. You call the cops, you'll never find out where she is."

"Okay, okay, I'm sorry. I'm just worried," Shy responded. "Well, where do we go from here?"

"Just stay by your phone. I'll talk to her today and let her know you're worried and that you really want to talk to her. That's all I can do. It's on her at that point. If Maya wants you to know where she is, she'll call. If not, there's nothing I can do about it."

"Well, I'm only gonna be in town for three or four more days, and then I'm leaving, so you've gotta make this quick."

"Oh, I didn't know you lived out of town," I replied,

playing it off.

"Tell her I miss her."

"I'll do that. Look, I gotta go. The nurse is here to give me some Percocet. I guess since I can't get a hit, this is the closet thing," I said, trying to keep up with the drug addict role.

Wasting no more time, I hung up. I still wasn't quite sure how I'd play this out, but I was sure for now I had the upper hand. As long as I could keep Shy in the dark, I would have time to figure out how to get exactly what I wanted out of her.

East Point Mall came into view up ahead. Once again I perked up, knowing money was near. A few minutes later, I was out of my car and sashaying across the parking lot's surface in my black Brian Atwood pumps and multi-print leggings that showcased my curves. I could see all the guys gawking at me as I made my way into the mall's entrance.

The food court was half filled when I arrived. As people conversed and ate, my eyes surveyed the entire court looking for Kendrick. Finally, I saw him sitting in the center of the court eating some Chinese food. Displaying a little smile, I headed through the maze of tables toward him. Once I reached his table, I sat down. Immediately, his glare at me glossed over with spite. His dislike for me showed all over his face. The crazy thing is, he looked a little surprised to see me.

"What are you doing here?" he questioned.

"What do you mean? Don't play stupid."

Kendrick quickly glanced again. "And why did we have to meet in such a public place? I'm a well known pastor. Some-one could see me and suspect something crazy."

"My game, my rules. Besides, you should've thought about those consequences when you were sticking your damn dick in an underage girl."

He glanced around again, hoping no one had heard me.

In all actuality, I'd told him to meet me there because I knew he wouldn't try anything crazy around a bunch of wit-nesses. I wasn't sure if he was going to be on some bullshit. If he was, I wasn't taking any chances. I wasn't going to let him catch me slipping like Vegas had.

"Now, fuck the small talk," I said, ready to get directly down to business. "Where's the money?"

He looked at me strangely. "What money?"

I chuckled. "Kendrick, don't play with me. I don't have time for games."

"I'm dead serious. What money?"

All out of patience, I placed my forearms on the table, and looked him dead in his face. "Muthafucka, I told you I'm not in the mood for games. Now, give me my fucking money or there will be problems."

"Look, I don't know what you're talking about. I gave your girl the money."

My girl, I thought to myself.

"What the hell are you talking about?" I asked, definitely wanting a better answer than he'd just given me.

"I just gave the money to your girl. She said you sent her."

"What girl? Who said I sent her?"

"Rasheeda."

My eyes widened. "Shit!" I screamed, causing the court's patrons to look at me. "Is this a joke?"

Embarrassed, Kendrick looked around, not appreciating having any attention brought to him. "No, it's not a joke. She called me yesterday and asked if I'd given you the money yet. When I told her no, and that I was meeting you here today, she just said okay and hung up. I thought you told her to call me."

"You stupid muthafucka! Why would I tell her to call you when we'd already talked? I haven't even spoken to Rasheeda," I snapped. "How long ago was she here?"

"She just left a minute before you got here."

I looked around to see if I could spot her. "What direction did she go?"

He pointed. "The door by the food court. If you came in

that way, I'm surprised you didn't see her."

Without another word said, I took off running in the direction, keeping my head on a swivel as I ran. Rasheeda was nowhere in sight though. When I made it to the parking lot, my eyes began to scan every car, every person. Unable to see her, I stood on my tippy toes, surveying the lot even harder. It was then that I saw the bitch's raggedy ass Jeep Cherokee several yards away at the light with her right blinker on. I knew she was headed to the freeway.

"You dirty bitch!" I screamed at the top of my lungs. "You sneaky, dirty bitch!"

Chapter 19-

Keema

Confidence totally had me this time. I'd made several drops and pickups over the past several days all by myself. Snake had been busy, but no one told me exactly what was keeping his time. All I'd been told was that I'd be rolling on my own for the time being, and since I was now the one taking *all* the risks, my cut of each drop would be bigger.

As far as Rocco, he told me he was limiting his visibility out here in the streets. He wouldn't tell me exactly why. He just said it was necessary. I wondered why, but accepted the position proudly because the more responsibility he gave me, the more it meant he trusted me. I was moving up the ranks faster than I'd expected. I knew then that it would be nothing to take Rocco away from Treasure. If I could get him to fuck with me this hard while I was disabled, I knew I would be able to turn his ass completely out once I could walk again.

At first, hitting these streets and making transactions with strangers had me nervous, in some instances scared. But I quickly realized just how respected in these streets Rocco's name was. Niggas knew better than to play with his money.

And since I was connected to him, they knew better than to play with me. That's why I was now comfortable rolling on my own. Yeah, I was taking one hell of a risk, but I knew it would be worth it in the end.

Underneath the bright shining sun, the car wash was nearly filled to capacity. Music blared loudly from freshly de-tailed whips; some old school, others newer models. Most sat on chromed out rims. Dope boys posted on their hoods sipping from styrofoam cups as a few women strolled the lot showing off their thick chocolate bodies, hoping to catch themselves a nigga with money.

Carwash employees with rags hanging from their belts and holding bottles of Windex, wax, and Armor All, maneu-vered through the lot also earning their pay and tips by provid-ing extra touches to each car. The white Tahoe sat off in a far corner of the lot. Through the maze of people and cars, I whirred towards the truck in my chair and stopped at the driver's side. Its tinted windows were up as Jay-Z's music played from inside. Within seconds, I was impatient. I knew they saw me waiting. Growing pissed, I banged on the door. The window came down.

"What the fuck is wrong wit' you?" the driver asked an-grily. He looked at the white boy sitting in the passenger seat. "This bitch trippin'."

They were the same two guys I'd made a transaction with before.

"Nigga, you saw me out here," I returned just as angry.

"Yeah *and*?"

"Well, that's disrespectful."

"Look, are we gonna do business or what?"

The white boy with the terrible acne stared at me. "Hey, where the fuck is Rocco? This is the second time he hasn't been around."

"Don't worry about that."

They glanced at each other again. The driver then

reached underneath his seat, pulled out his Glock and pointed it directly in my face. "Who the fuck do you think you're talkin' to?" he asked. "Don't you know that I'll murk your ass right here? Don't play wit' me."

I didn't say anything. My eyes were directly on the gun, scared it would go off at any second.

"Now, my home boy asked you a question. Where the fuck is Rocco?"

A lump developed in my throat. Nervousness took over me, but I realized and remembered that Rocco's name carried weight in these streets. That realization made me swallow the lump and say defiantly, "Look, muthafucka, I don't have time for games. I've got shit to do and people to see. Fuck dealing with Rocco. You deal with me now or you don't deal with any-body."

Both men were silent. A hint of surprise registered on their faces.

"Rocco has stepped down. I'm running this shit now. So, either put that gun down and do business or I'm leaving."

Neither man knew quite how to take me. My fearless-ness caught them off guard. If they only knew, though. In all honesty, I was scared to death. I just refused to show it. One thing I'd learned while making drops and pickups is that niggas were like wolves. They could smell fear. Obviously, with these two fools, I had to put my mack hand down and let them know that this shit wasn't a game. If I didn't, we'd be going through this ridiculous routine every time we had to deal with each other. They would probably even take shit further; like trying to rob me. Either way, I wasn't having it.

When the two dudes still didn't say anything, I gave them one last chance. "So, what's up? Are we gonna do busi-ness or what?"

The driver finally placed the gun to his side. "I told you the last time to tell Rocco if the plans changed to let me know."

"Well, I guess he didn't get a chance to call. Besides, do

you think he would've made me his right hand bitch if I couldn't be trusted?"

Of course Treasure was still the closest thing to his right-hand bitch for the moment, but these two dudes didn't have to know. Besides, I really would be holding that title very soon.

"Do you muthafuckas think Rocco would be fucking with me if he thought I was a cop?" I continued.

Both men looked at each other skeptically then back at me. That was it. They were wasting too much time. I had shit to do. "Look," I said. "When y'all niggas are finally ready to do business, call me."

I then turned my chair around and began to roll away.

"Hold up!" the driver called out.

I stopped.

"Let's get this shit done!"

"Bout damn time," I said, turning back around.

"Let me see the work."

"No, this ain't going down like it did last time. Let me see the money first."

"What, you think we ain't got it or something?" the driver asked.

"I don't know what y'all got. All I know is I need to see some money first. Just like y'all don't trust me, I don't trust you either."

He looked at me for a moment then turned to nod to his partner. At that moment, the white guy tossed a bag to him. He then handed the bag to me. I looked inside and saw nothing but stacks of hundreds.

"Is it all here?" I asked, looking at them suspiciously.

"Of course."

"It better be. If it ain't, that's your ass."

"Man, whatever. Where's the shit?"

I looked around swiftly to make sure no one was watching us. Seeing the coast was clear, I pulled out a bag that contained one kilo and handed it to him. Moments later, I turned around and rolled back to my van.

Before riding out, I had to sit for a moment and stare at the money on my lap. It appeared to be about fifty thousand dollars. With my cut and money I'd saved, I could finally send the doctor over in the Dominican the entire deposit. I was finally gonna be able to walk again. The thought brought a huge smile to my face. I was going to send the money off first thing tomorrow morning. Damn, I couldn't wait.

All of a sudden, my cell phone rang. Seeing the number pop up on the screen caught me completely by surprise. It was Treasure. The two of us hadn't spoken since our fallout. I still didn't want to talk to her ass and still hadn't forgiven her for putting her damn hands on me, but I answered anyway, figuring it might have something to do with business.

"What?" I answered coldly.

"Look, I didn't call you to argue or to even have a fucking family reunion," she said. "Actually, I'm still pissed about you stealing my damn money."

"Listen, I didn't steal your money, so stop saying that shit."

"So, you're gonna go to the grave with that lie, huh?"

"I thought you didn't call me to argue. What do you want, Treasure?"

"I called because I've got something important to tell you."

Just hearing her voice made me despise her even more. Its sound made my blood boil. I knew it was unnatural to hate my daughter, but I couldn't help it. She was too much like me.

"Well, talk. What is it?"

"Not over the phone. We need to meet up somewhere A.S.A.P."

A smile crept across my lips. With the plan that me and Toy had, having Treasure meet me at the vacant house where Maya's body was rotting was gonna be easier than I thought.

"Yeah, that's cool. Meet me near Westport. I will be

at…"

"No, I can't come over there. I don't have time," she interrupted. "Meet me at that Wendy's on York Road."

I didn't want her to be suspicious so I let it go…for now. "When?"

"Right now."

"Alright, I'm on my way."

Hanging up, I turned the key in the ignition and headed out. Twenty minutes later, I pulled up to Wendy's and headed straight to the drive thru. After grabbing something to eat, I parked and waited. Five minutes later, Treasure's car pulled up beside me. She shut off the engine, hopped out and jumped into my van's passenger seat.

I glared at her while taking a bite of my spicy chicken sandwich.

She studied the van's interior. "I heard you got a van."

"Yup," I replied proudly. "You hate it, don't you? You hate the fact that I don't have to ask your ass for a ride anymore, huh?"

"Ma, I could care less."

I rolled my eyes at her. "You're such a damn hater, Treasure. Look at me." I pointed to my hair that I'd just gotten done earlier that morning. "I look good, don't I?"

Treasure sighed. "Why are you trying to start with me? I didn't come here for this." She looked at her watch like she was in a rush.

"So, what so you want, Treasure? I've got shit to handle anyway."

Treasure shook her head. "Frenchie and Shy are back in town."

All the color drained from my face at the sound of those two names. I looked at my daughter closely.

"Yeah, I thought you'd react that way," she said.

"How do you know they're back in town?"

"Because I saw them."

"What the fuck do you mean you saw them?" She wasn't giving me enough details.

"It means, I *saw* them. I saw their asses with my own two eyes."

I thought she was joking. "Treasure, get out of my van. I don't have time for these childish ass games."

"I'm not joking. I put it on Cash's and grandma's life."

I looked at her super seriously. Anytime she truly meant something, she'd put it on the lives of the two people she truly loved.

"You're serious?" I asked.

"Yeah, you know I don't play like that."

I could feel my heart began to pump a little faster. "Where did you see them?"

Treasure informed me that she couldn't exactly say where they were yet. She then began to tell me all about the Vegas situation since that was what lead up to her seeing Frenchie and Shy. She also included all the details about Maya's kidnapping and her thinking Toy had let them go. I played stupid of course and acted like I didn't know anything. She even told me about Vegas' murder. None of it really peaked my interest though. I was much more interested in Frenchie and Shy.

"Have you spoken to Toy?" she asked me.

"Nah, why would I talk to her?"

"I don't know. I've been trying to reach her lately and she hasn't been answering. I thought she might've stopped by the house or something."

I shook my head back and forth. "I haven't heard from her."

"When I catch that bitch, her ass is as good as dead." Treasure looked at her watch again. "I gotta get to school. I got something to handle."

"Wait a minute. What about Frenchie and Shy?"

"Don't worry about it. We can meet up later tonight and

come up with a plan."

"But…"

"I said we can meet up later. I gotta go!"

At that point, Treasure hopped out of the van, got into her car and pulled off leaving me to my own thoughts and worries. Remembering that I had to hit a couple of Rocco's stash houses to pick up more work, I cranked up the van and pulled out of the lot. As I headed to the spot, all I could think about was that day on the sidewalk. I could still see myself lying there. I could still feel the blood pooling around me. I could still feel the bullet tearing through my flesh. The memory wouldn't allow me to break free from it.

Sitting at a stop light, I leaned back in my seat and mindlessly looked up into the rearview mirror and saw a black Mustang GT directly behind me. When the light turned green, I pulled off. As I drove, the reason why I'd been placed into my wheelchair wouldn't release its grip on me, and knowing Frenchie and Shy were back in town brought it all back. No matter how many corners I bent or how many faces I passed, the brutal memory wouldn't stop stressing me.

I was several blocks away from the spot when I stopped at another light. Once again, my eyes drifted to the rearview mirror, and once again, I saw the same black Mustang behind me. I looked a little closer at the mirror, thinking maybe my eyes were deceiving me or maybe it wasn't the same car. Seconds later, the light turned green. I pulled away while glancing back and forth from the mirror to the street ahead of me. Sure enough…the car stayed directly behind me.

I began to tell myself maybe I was worrying for nothing. Maybe the car just happened to be headed in the same direction. It would pull away at any moment and head on about its business. Fearfully though, I realized there was only one way to find out…

I immediately made a left turn.

My eyes rose to the mirror again and watched as the corner faded further and further behind me. Suddenly, the car appeared and made the same turn causing me to sit up in my seat and grip the steering wheel tightly. I then made a right turn. I watched the rearview nervously and once again the car made the exact same turn. It was obvious now that I was being followed.

My heart began to race. *How long had the car been following me*, I wondered. Who was it? Could it be Frenchie and Shy? Had they found me just that quick? The thought scared the shit out of me. Abruptly, another possibility entered my mind. Could it be the cops? Had they seen me back at the carwash? I had no idea who it was. The thought of me still being on probation, had me nervous as hell. All I knew was I wasn't going to allow whoever it was to catch me.

Chapter 20-

Treasure

The driver of the other car slammed on her brakes and hit the horn as I sped my Benz into the parking space she attempted to pull into. As if nothing happened, I hopped out of my car and headed toward my school's entrance; never giving her a second look.

"I was going to park there!" the woman shouted.

"Does it look like I care?" I yelled back, never losing a step.

The closer I got to the door, the more I steamed. I couldn't believe Rasheeda would play me like that. I also couldn't believe she had the heart to do something so foul. She knew my pedigree. She knew I wasn't the scared type. She knew I would get her ass back at any cost. That's what made it so hard to believe. Shit, if I hadn't seen it for myself, I wouldn't have believed it.

Within seconds, I snatched the front door open and stormed down the hallway. The sharp heels of my shoes echoed loudly off the walls and rows of lockers. My face twisted into something far from a scowl. The look was pure evil. I wanted

Rasheeda's ass badly.

Catching Rasheeda here was most likely a long shot, I'd already figured. Her mother was a strict disciplinarian and was always on Rasheeda about school and keeping her grades up. Because of that, despite fucking for money, Rasheeda *never* missed a day of school. But Rasheeda knew I didn't play games about my cash. She knew I would whoop her ass and school would be the first place I'd looked for her. Either way, I wasn't leaving any stones unturned. I was going to search high and low for that thieving bitch, regardless of what it took. I thought about the box cutter that I'd slipped in my Gucci messenger bag. Since I couldn't get to my gun, I'd picked up the next best thing. Once again, when I caught up to Rasheeda, she was gonna give me my money or else.

I shoved open another door and stomped up the staircase to the second floor. As soon as I stepped out into the hallway, I saw a few fellow students leaning against their lockers cutting class. Immediately, their eyes landed on me. It was like that anytime I came to school. I set the standards for dressing, talking and walking. My swag was legendary.

"Hey, Treasure," a girl said, trying to act like she was cool with me.

Ignoring her, I kept walking

With a smirk on his face, a dude asked snidely, "What brings you here?"

"Definitely not your broke, dusty ass," I told him and walked past. "Oh, yeah by the way, those Jordans you got on came out *last year*. So, step your game up before you talk to me."

Satisfied that I'd put his lame ass in his place, I arrived at my Algebra 2 class. When I snatched the door open and walked inside, my teacher, Mrs. Beckman, stopped her lesson in midsentence. My eyes scoured the class for Rasheeda. I didn't see her.

"Well, well, are you finally joining us today, Ms.

Newell?" Mrs. Beckman asked, clearly offended that I'd disrupted the class. "If so, have a seat."

Ignoring her, I continued scouring the class just in case Rasheeda was simply ducking down in a seat behind someone. Hell, I looked for Toy, too since she was in the same class. Killing two birds with one stone would've been rewarding.

"Treasure, have a seat," Mrs. Beckman instructed again.

"Where's Rasheeda?"

She looked at me like I was insane. "Excuse me?"

"Rasheeda, have you seen her?"

"Treasure, I'm not sure where you left your manners. But I would appreciate it if you would either take a seat or exit my classroom. Either decision is clearly up to you."

"Did she come to school today?" I wasn't going to leave until I got my answers.

"No, she's absent today."

"Well, what about Toy?" I continued to question.

"She's absent as well. As a matter of fact, she's been absent as long as you have. Now, for the last time, have a seat," Mrs. Beckman responded.

I instantly became frustrated.

"Treasure, do you know where you're going to end up without an education; where you'll be if you don't graduate?"

I finally looked at my teacher who looked like she was in her early fifties.

"Getting an education exposes you to way more alternatives in life. If you don't have one, there's a limited amount of things that you'll be able to accomplish."

"Look, Mrs. Beckman, I don't have time for any of your sermons right now."

With a look of disbelief, she said, "Well, the students in here at this moment are interested in learning. If that doesn't fit your mold, you need…"

Unable to take anymore preaching, I snapped. "Does it look like I'm here to fucking learn? Can't you see that I'm looking for someone?"

What little bit of color Mrs. Beckam's pale white face held quickly disappeared.

A bunch of "Oohhhs" and "Ahhhhs" came from the students as they watched me, curious of what disrespect I would conjure up next.

"That's it. I'm not tolerating that type of behavior in my classroom." She pointed to the door. "Get out! And don't think I'm not going to inform, Mr. Davidson about this."

"Yeah, whatever," I replied. I could care less what she told our principal.

I shrugged her off and walked out of the classroom wondering where I would search for Rasheeda next. At the moment she was all I could think about. Her and my damn money.

"Treasure!" someone suddenly called out to me from behind. I turned to see one of my Algebra 2 classmates rushing down the hall towards me.

"Look, I'm busy," I said. "I ain't got time to talk."

"It's about Rocco."

Hearing Rocco's name made me stop and turn. "What about Rocco?" I asked as she reached me.

"There are some things you really need to know about him."

"Like what?" My face twisted. What the fuck did she know about *my* man?

"Treasure…" she attempted.

"Brianna!" Mrs. Beckman yelled, interrupting her. "Unless you want to be suspended, I suggest you get back in this classroom."

Quickly, Brianna reached into her pocket, pulled out a small piece of paper and stuffed it in the palm of my hand. "This is my number," she told me. "Call me as soon as school is over."

"But…"

She turned and jogged back to class. Once she was inside, Mrs. Beckman rolled her eyes at me and slammed the door, leaving me in the hallway alone. Automatically my brain started wondering what was up. What the hell did Brianna know about Rocco that I didn't? Had she seen him cheating on me? The questions were coming a mile a minute.

However, knowing I had to deal with the Rasheeda situation first, I stuffed the number into my pocket and headed down the hall to the door that led to the staircase. As I rapidly made my way, all of a sudden a girl came out of nowhere and stepped directly in my path. I stopped.

"What's good, Treasure?" she asked with a sick smile on her face.

I recognized her immediately. She was the tall, dark-skinned chick from my Sweet 16 party who hadn't been invited.

A second later, I heard footsteps making their way behind me. When I turned around, the other girl from my party appeared. I watched carefully as she made her way beside her partner in crime. As pissed as I was, if they had any intentions on jumping me, I was certainly gonna give them a run for their money today.

"Told you we'd see your ass again," the taller, nappy headed one told me.

"Look, get the fuck out of my way. I don't have time for this," I said, glancing back and forth at both of them. "And I ain't in the mood."

"You think we give a fuck about what you got time for?" the taller girl asked. She stepped to me. "You know you're gonna get what's comin' to you, right?"

"Yeah, it's only a matter of time," the other girl co-signed.

Since I was outnumbered, I placed my hand inside my bag, ready to go for the box cutter. Jealous bitches like them were relentless, so I had to be prepared. I wasn't going out like a fool.

Suddenly, a door opened and Mr. Ferris, the gym teacher

appeared. "Why aren't you ladies in class?" he inquired. "Break that up."

As soon as they saw him, both girls quickly darted past me and made their way back down the hall. I could hear Mr. Ferris saying something else to me as I turned around and made my way back outside. If he thought I was about to sit there and listen to his nonsense, he was sadly mistaken. Seconds later, I was in my car and headed back to the hood.

It only took fifteen minutes to get to Rasheeda's neighborhood. I slowly pulled in front of her house, but didn't see her car. Her mother's car wasn't around either, meaning she was most likely at work. Pulling away from the curb, I headed around the hood to some of the spots I knew Rasheeda frequented; the nail salon, the Chinese carry out and a few other places. No luck, though. I came up blank each time.

"Fuck!" I screamed, banging on the steering wheel.

I was past furious. Rasheeda had lightened my damn pockets and now she was nowhere to be found. I wanted to kill her. I told myself I refused to take a loss and grabbed the phone to call Kendrick. Someone was going to make this shit right. And since I couldn't get hold of Rasheeda, it was going to have to be him.

"Pastor Kendrick Morris," he answered with a phony tone.

"I want my money."

He paused for a moment. "I'm in the middle of a missionary meeting."

"Do you think I give a fuck about what your snake ass in the middle of? I said I want my money!"

"Hold on a second."

I listened carefully to what was going on as Kendrick told someone in the background that he had to take this important call. "Please excuse me for a brief moment," I heard him say. A few seconds passed.

"Look, I gave you your damn money," Kendrick finally

said, getting back on the phone. I'm pretty sure he was out of earshot of his congregation.

"No, nigga. You gave *my* money to Rasheeda."

"And?"

"I didn't authorize that shit. I didn't tell you to give her my money."

"Look, that's between you and her. I did my part. Our agreement is over and done, so stop bothering me. I have nothing else to do with this situation."

"Listen here, muthafucka. You have *everything* to do with this situation. And you're gonna continue to have everything to do with it until I say otherwise."

Kendrick sighed. "Treasure, let me say this as calmly as possible. Like I said, I did my part by giving you the money. It's not my fault that your friend got to it before you did. Maybe the next time you should communicate a little bit better with your employees."

"But I never communicated with her. I never told her to meet you there!" I roared.

"Well, that's your loss and definitely not my problem. You and I are done."

I saw red instantly. I couldn't believe that this pedophile muthafucka was trying to play me. I couldn't believe that he was being so cocky. Didn't he know that I could destroy him? Didn't he know that I could ruin his life? I wanted so badly to go hard on him and scream to the top of my lungs about needing my cash. But something told me to fall back. Something told me to handle the situation in a totally different manner.

"You're right, Kendrick." It took everything within me to hold my composure. "I'm sorry for even calling you about this. Everything will be okay once I find, Rasheeda and work this out."

"Good, now lose my number," he said just before the line went dead.

At that moment all I could do was chuckle. "Muthafucka, you're crazy if you think you're not gonna pay for that mistake."

A few minutes later, I pulled up to my house. Since the fallout with my mother, I'd been staying with Rocco in a hotel. Not only did I need to pack some clothes, I mainly needed my laptop. After pulling into the driveway, I jumped out with a serious mission to complete. When I got to the front door, I stuck my key inside the lock only to find out that it wouldn't turn. I pulled the key out. After looking down to make sure I had the correct one, I tried it once again, but it still wouldn't work.

"What the hell?"

I banged on the door with both fists hoping that Shane wasn't at his job. Thoughts of why the locks had been changed rushed in my head as I kept banging. Seconds later, I could hear the lock being opened. When Shane opened the door, he smiled at me immediately and started clapping his hands.

"Treasure come home!" he stated happily. "Treasure come home!"

"Treasure come home, my ass!" I said, brushing past him. "What's wrong with the locks, Shane? Why couldn't I use my key?"

"Treasure come home," he said once again.

"Shane, what happened to the locks?" I yelled. I gave him an expression that meant I wasn't playing around.

"Keema change locks."

"What?"

Shane just gave me one of those simple looks only he could give.

"I still pay the bills up in this muthafucka! I still keep food in the fridge, the lights and the gas on! What gives her the right to change some damn locks?"

Shane obviously didn't know what to say. He just stood there.

I looked over his shoulder to see that the new deadbolt lock was one that even prevented a person from getting out without a key.

"When did she put that lock on the door?" I questioned him.

"Yesterday."

"Why?"

Shane just shrugged his shoulders.

"Wait until I see her ass later on," I said fuming.

Deciding not to let the lock situation get me more furious than I already was, I turned around and headed to my room to get what I came for. My bedroom was still trashed. Stepping over clothes and shoes, I grabbed my laptop from the dresser and tossed it onto my bed. Grabbing a purse that I hadn't carried with me in over a week, I reached inside and pulled out my flip camera. After booting up the computer, I inserted the flip cam's USB drive. Seconds later, I was looking at the footage of Kendrick's nasty rendezvous with Rasheeda. A twisted smile appeared on my face.

"So, you thought I was playing with your ass, huh?" I said as Kendrick stroked his dick inside Rasheeda over and over again. "It's my loss, huh? Alright, nigga, watch my moves."

Turning off the video, I went online to find the e-mail addresses to several different Baltimore detectives along with a local news station. I then went to my fake gmail account, composed a new message and typed *"LOCAL PASTOR, KENDRICK MORRIS SLEEPS WITH AN UNDERAGE GIRL,"* in the subject line. I was beyond excited as I attached the file, then hit the red send button.

"Mission accomplished," I said, completely satisfied with what I'd done.

After grabbing a few outfits along with some shoes and underwear, I also grabbed a suitcase, and my laptop, then headed out my door. As I got closer to the living room, I suddenly heard a little boy say, "No, I want my mommy!"

My eyes increased. I couldn't believe what I'd just heard

as I stopped in midstride and turned around. "What the fuck?" I said, realizing the voice had come from Shane's room.

I couldn't get to Shane's room fast enough. When I pushed open his door, Shane was sitting on his bed trying to feed Maya's son some tuna fish fresh out of the can. My mouth dropped.

"No!" Jaden wailed. "I don't want it! I want my mommy!"

"Keema said you need to eat," Shane responded.

"Shane, how did he get here?"

At that moment, Maya's son obviously remembered what I'd done to his mother before because he quickly got up from the bed and backed against the wall, never allowing his eyes to leave me.

"Toy and him spent the night," Shane answered.

I couldn't believe my fucking ears. "What do you mean him and Toy spent the night?"

"They spend the night. Keema brought them. They spend the night," Shane repeated.

The shit was the craziest thing I'd heard in my life. Not only did Toy betray and lie to me, but my own mother was now in cahoots with the bitch, too. I couldn't believe she'd just lied to my face and told me that she hadn't spoken with Toy. I suddenly wondered where Maya was. This shit was playing out just like a scene in a bad movie.

"Where's Toy now?"

"Keema leave. Toy leave." Shane stood up and looked at Jaden. "Keema said you need to eat."

"Those trifling bitches!" I yelled, then began to pace the floor. "Those low down, dirty, trifling bitches!"

At that moment I thought I'd heard it all. I thought nothing more could be said to infuriate me. I couldn't have been more wrong though. What Shane said next floored me...

"Treasure, Keema suck Rocco's dick."

Chapter 21-

Keema

The sun had fallen, leaving darkness to follow closely behind in its footsteps, but I was still like the Energizer Bunny. I'd been grinding all day for Rocco and didn't even want to slow down. Although confined to a wheelchair, I was getting back to what always use to bring me joy…

Chasing money!

Damn, it felt great to be back at something I'd always been good at. It was like a natural high each time I felt bill after bill in the palm of my hand. I loved it. I missed having that feeling, but now it was back; feeling like it had never left. I was independent again.

The most beautiful thing about it all though was that earlier today I was able to stop by the bank and wire the twenty-five thousand dollar deposit for my surgery. I caught the bank just as it was about to close. It was obvious the teller was anxious to lock the doors and go home. I didn't give a fuck, though. A pack of wild horses wasn't going to keep me up out of there. I wasn't going to wait another second to send the money off. I needed to walk.

First thing the following morning, I was going to call the doctor and schedule my first consultation. From there, I would hop on the computer, hit the internet and book myself a plane ticket. I couldn't wait. I could already feel the Dominican sun on my face. I'd never been outside the country, so I also had to get an expedited passport. With my probation almost up, I'm pretty sure my probation officer wouldn't mind me leaving to go handle some major shit such as this. Even if she didn't, I was going anyway. At this point, I'd come too damn far to let any-thing or anyone stop me from reaching my goal.

Before I did any of that though, I had to get with Rocco in the morning and give him his cut from all the drops and pick ups I'd made today. Honestly, the thought crossed my mind to skim a little cheese off the top. Some of the niggas I'd come across today looked like major pussies. They looked like I could easily taken a thousand here or there from their payments and then lied to Rocco, telling him they'd shorted him. The thought was on my mind super heavy. I was extremely tempted, but chose not to. For now anyway.

But despite my happiness, Frenchie and Shy kept find-ing their way inside my head. Those muthafuckas were the rea-son I'd been placed in this position in the first place. They were the reason for my pain, sadness and misery. Now, it was pay-back time. It was time the two of them got a chance to see what it was like to hurt.

I thought seriously about what I wanted to do with them, but couldn't come up with a decision. I didn't know if I wanted to outright kill them, torture them or maybe cripple the both of them like they'd done to me. However it went down, I defi-nitely wanted revenge. Whatever the fuck it was going to be, it was going to be crucial. I was absolutely sure of that. I was ready for war.

Suddenly, a text came through my phone. While keeping an eye on the road ahead of me, I grabbed my cell from the cup holder and quickly looked down. It was from Treasure.

You trifling foul ass bitch! I can't believe you. Shane told me every thing! You sucked Rocco's dick? Wait 'till I see you!

"Shane, you son of a bitch!" I yelled after reading the message. "You dumb, retarded muthafucka!"

I was furious. The point of giving him some pussy was to keep him quiet and he still told.

"Niggas can never just hit the pussy and keep the shit quiet," I said like someone was in the car listening.

When I got home, I was gonna go hard on his ass. But for now, I had to smooth things over with Treasure. She had the information I needed on Frenchie and Shy. We were even supposed to be meeting up to discuss it. I needed the chance to get the revenge I'd waited on for so long. Promptly, I went to my recent call list. But before I could hit her name, Snake's name and number appeared on the screen.

"Snake, I'm busy right now," I told him as soon as I answered. "I'll have to…"

"Fuck that," he replied with an attitude. "Whatever you doin' right now, put an end to that shit."

"Why?"

"Because I need you to come switch places with me."

"Switch places with you? What are you talking about?"

"Stop askin' questions, Keema and just do it. I gotta make some moves."

"Well, whatever the hell you're talking about, why can't you get somebody else to do it? I really have…"

"Look, Keema, I need you to get over here to The Aloft in Arundel Mills right now. It's just that plain and simple. Besides, it's 'cause of you that I'm here in the first fuckin' place. Shit, you need to be here handlin' your own problems."

"What does that mean?"

"I'm pretty sure you talked to Treasure by now. You already know that Rocco got me watchin' that nigga who you had beef with and his girl."

Snake didn't have to say another word before it hit me. The hotel must've been where Frenchie and Shy were.

"I'll be there in twenty minutes," I said, ending the call.

Anxiously, I slammed my foot down on the gas pedal. I drove to the hotel so fast, by the time I whipped into the parking lot several minutes later my van was smoking. Eyeing Snake's Escalade, when I parked beside him, he hopped out of his truck and jumped inside.

"I been here for two damn days watchin' these muthafuckas!" Snake ranted as soon as he closed the door. "Do you know how much money I've missed out on? I can't believe Rocco put me on this dumb shit."

"Has Rocco been here?" I asked, not the least bit interested in Snake's problems.

"Yeah, he dropped by last night to switch cars with me and bring me somethin' to eat."

"So, they haven't left… not even once?"

"I followed the dude earlier. He left to go to The Cheesecake Factory across the street, but he came right back though," Snake answered. "I never saw the chick, so I guess she stayed in the hotel."

"What's he driving?"

Snake pointed. "The white Range Rover over there."

I glanced at it and immediately grew evil, knowing Frenchie had spent my fucking money on the brand new truck. I could see him and Shy riding around in that muthafucka like love birds. The shit made me sick to my stomach.

Looking at me suspiciously, Snake asked, "So, those are the fools who put you in that wheelchair, huh?"

I didn't answer. I just watched the hotel's entrance.

"What did you do to them?"

"That's not important right now."

"To me it is. Shit, if I'm out here puttin' myself in harm's way, I'd like to at least know why."

"Well, I don't want to talk about it right now and I'm *not* going to talk about it. Besides, that's not important."

Snake shrugged me off. "Whatever, suit yourself. I got shit to do." He reached for the door handle. "By the way, how many drops have you done since I been here?"

I never took my eyes away from the hotel. "Why is that so important right now?"

"Because I wanna know how much money you been gettin' while I been sittin' out this muthafucka, that's why. You shoulda been here doin' this shit, not me!"

"You mad because Rocco demoted you?" I chuckled.

"I didn't get demoted bitch…trust me," Snake fired back.

I glanced at him for a second. "Well, I'll let Rocco tell you that information if he wishes to share."

"You know what, fuck you, Keema," Snake responded. He grabbed the door handle again.

An idea crossed my mind, which made me grab his arm. "Wait a minute."

Looking at my hand like it had shit stuck to it, Snake flaunted an evil glare. "What do you want?"

"You wanna make some money?"

Snake looked at me more suspiciously than before. "How?"

"Help me kill these muthafuckas."

He finally smiled. "Are you serious?"

"Very."

"What do you need my help for?"

As if it wasn't obvious, I said, "Look at me," while holding my arms out. "How effective could I be?"

He looked at me, but didn't say anything.

"Snake, I know you don't fuck with me. I know you don't like me. Shit, nigga, I don't like your ass either, but I really need your help."

He still didn't look too eager to help me out.

"Alright," I said, grabbing the bag full of money. I

reached inside and counted out ten thousand dollars. "This is ten, nigga; my cut for the day. It's yours if you do this for me."

Of course my twenty-five thousand dollar cut was already sitting in some bank in The Dominican Republic right now. But I couldn't miss out on this opportunity. I'd just have to make it up to Rocco later on.

Snake's eyes studied the money. I could tell the wheels inside his head were now spinning. He understood the language of money just like me. "Alright," he finally said. "But you can't tell Rocco I did this shit."

"What, you can only kill for him or something?" When I noticed that Snake didn't find my comment too funny, I replied with, "No problem."

He took the money.

I smiled.

"What you smilin' for? Don't get shit twisted. I'm not doin' this for you. I'm doin' it for the money. There's a big difference."

"Understood. Now, how are we gonna do this?"

"So, you don't have a plan?"

"No."

Snake shook his head. "A fuckin' amateur. We'll figure something out. Give me a minute, though. I gotta go use the bathroom, and I'm tired of pissin' outside."

With that said, Snake got out of the van and headed to the hotel's entrance. I then called Toy. I'd been meaning to get with her ever since Shane texted me earlier today. It had skipped my mind until now.

"Yeah," she answered dryly.

"First of all, Shane texted me and told me you left right after I did this morning and didn't come back. Where are you?"

There was a silence. I hated silences in conversations like this one. It usually meant the person was trying to come up with a lie.

"I had to handle something important," she finally said.

"Like what?"

"Just something."

I didn't like the way that sounded.

"Toy, don't even think about leaving that little boy at my damn house. This is your mess, you understand?"

"It's not like that, Keema. I wouldn't do no shit like that."

"Yeah, whatever. Anyway, I need you to come meet me somewhere."

"Where?"

"The Aloft Hotel. The one out in Arundel Mills."

"Why?"

"Don't worry about the whys. Just get here. I need you to do something." Although I didn't have a concrete plan, I figured Toy could help Snake out if he needed some backup. There was only so much I could do.

She paused.

"Is there a problem?"

"I just don't understand why you'd need me."

"Look, Toy, didn't I come through for your ass? Didn't I help you clean up your little mess?"

"Yeah," she answered hesitantly.

"Alright then. I need you to get here now and help me take care of something important. And don't worry, your role will be minimal. I already paid my boy Snake to do the hard part."

She sighed with annoyance like I was getting on her nerves.

"Toy, this isn't a request and it isn't up for discussion. Just like I helped you, I need you to help me, do you understand?"

She sighed again, then finally said, "Alright."

"I'm in the parking lot waiting," I told her before hanging up.

As soon as I sat the phone down on the console, a text

came through. Picking the phone up again, I saw the text was
from Ms. Kyle asking me to call her. Obviously having no time
for her at the moment, I sat the phone back down. Right now,
my mind was focused on Frenchie and Shy.

Leaning back into the seat, I kept my eyes on the entrance. About fifteen minutes passed by. There was no movement. Snake hadn't even come back. As I began to wonder what
was taking him so long, a Pizza Hut delivery car pulled into the
lot. It stopped at the hotel's entrance. I watched as a young delivery boy hopped out with a pizza box in his hand and headed
inside. Seeing that shit, immediately made my stomach growl. I
hadn't eaten in hours and could've used some energy. As I
thought about stopping the guy on his way out to see if he
would sell me one, another text came through my phone. It was
from Snake.

It's on. Come to room 320.

I got off the elevator at the third floor and began rolling
down the carpeted hallway towards room 320. Everything was
silent. I couldn't help beginning to feel nervous. Although I'd
paid Snake, there was no guarantee that he would be loyal.
After all, he didn't like me and never had any problems showing it. I was now wondering if maybe he'd just taken my money
and started fucking with Frenchie and Shy. Maybe he'd called
me up to put a hole in my head while Frenchie and Shy
watched. All types of thoughts went through my mind.

The trip down the hallway seemed like forever. While
my heart rate raced, my palms were drenched in sweat. A lump
filled my throat. Once I finally reached the room, I placed my
ear to the door. I heard nothing. For a moment, I just sat there
afraid to knock. I was scared to death of what might possibly be
waiting on the other side. A part of me wanted to turn around;
to go back to my van until I could be sure that Snake wasn't

lying. But the other part of me wanted to get this shit over with. Where the fuck was Toy? She had yet to call; telling me that she'd arrived. I could've sent her in the room first; using her ass as a shield.

After building up enough nerve, I knocked, dreading the moment it opened. Within a couple seconds, the door opened up slowly, and Snake's face appeared from behind it. I couldn't see the rest of his body or anything behind him.

"Come in," he said and opened the door fully exposing the gun in his hand.

It was at that moment when I saw both Frenchie and Shy at the far end of the room. Both were sitting on the bed. Shy was crying while Frenchie just sat there with an evil look on his face.

I rolled inside and Snake shut the door behind me. Strangely, I didn't know what to say. I could only look at Frenchie and Shy in silence. My moment had finally come and I could only sit there with a loss for words.

"So, what do you want me to do with them?" Snake pointed at both of them with his gun.

I stared at Frenchie, realizing that he'd gained a lot of weight since four years ago. Shy on the other hand, still looked the same. Same thick ass eyebrows…same crazy eyes that didn't seem to blink too often.

"How did you find out what room they were in?" I asked Snake.

"I was comin' out of the bathroom, and it just so happened that the nigga was downstairs in the lobby payin' for a pizza. I then overheard the nigga tell the front desk clerk that housekeepin' didn't come clean room 320 today." Snake smiled. "I mean how easy was that shit?"

I glanced at the pizza box sitting on the bed.

"We don't have time to be bullshittin' though, Keema. What do you want done?" Snake continued.

He began slipping a silencer onto the tip of his gun.

I looked at my enemies.

"Keema, I'm sorry," Shy pleaded, knowing she was staring at the final moments of her life. "Please don't kill us." Tears streamed down her face.

"Don't beg that bitch," Frenchie said.

"But I don't wanna die," Shy responded.

Snake raised his gun. "Sshhh. Lower your fuckin' voice!"

"You should've thought about that before you stole my money and put me in this chair," I told her heartlessly.

"Stole *your* money?" Frenchie looked displeased. "Bitch, that was *my* fuckin' money. It was never yours from the start. You were just holdin' it for me."

He was right about that, but it made no difference to me.

"As far as the chair, consider yourself lucky. I meant to kill you. Evidently the bullet missed the vital organs," Frenchie added.

His words were said with a sneer. He had no compassion for what he'd done to me.

"You son of a bitch!' I spewed. "You took my fucking legs!"

"And you took my brother's life!" he shouted just as loudly and angrily. "You took what I loved away from me so you deserve that chair. Shit, your ass deserved to die! Don't you see that you're the reason why this all happened? Don't you see what role you played in this shit? "

"Look, I don't mean to disturb this little family reunion shit y'all got goin' on, but, Keema, we don't have a lot of time. Do you want them dead or not?" Snake interrupted.

Shy dropped to her knees. "No, Keema. Please don't. Please don't."

Frenchie said nothing. He was defiant to the end.

My decision had been made a long time ago. I finally looked at Snake and gave him my answer…

"Kill them."

Just like the gangsta he was, I watched as Snake took aim at Shy's face and pulled the trigger. Her body fell back into the bed within seconds.

"Fuck you, nigga!" Frenchie yelled. "Fuck you and that bitch! Fuck…"

Snake squeezed the trigger.

Instead of falling on the bed, Frenchie's body hit the floor with a hard thump.

My revenge had finally been served.

Chapter 22-
Keema

    Fuck the fact that he was Autistic. Fuck the fact that he had nowhere else to go. Fuck the fact that these streets would eat his black ass alive. None of that meant anything to me. In my book, he'd crossed me and there was no coming back from that.

    Shane stood outside with a simple look on his face, finding it hard to comprehend what exactly was happening. Repeatedly, I rolled past his goofy looking ass with piles of his clothes on my lap. Each time I reached the wheelchair ramp, I tossed them out onto the lawn.

    "You snitching ass muthafucka," I told him as I rolled by with the latest load.

    "Keema mad at me?" he asked.

    "What do you think? Ain't no fat, disloyal muthafucka gonna be living up in my house, eating my food, watching my cable and wiggling his crusty ass toes underneath my air conditioning."

    As I turned to go back in the house, he blocked my way. "Keema mad at…"

"Move, Shane!"

"Keema."

"I said move, Shane! Move now or I'll run your ass over!"

He stepped to the side with tears in his eyes.

Ignoring his sadness, I rolled inside, got the last of his clothes and came back out. As I heaved them onto the lawn, Shane pitifully asked, "Keema not suck Shane's wee-wee no more?"

I was furious. "Quit lying. I never sucked your damn dick!"

Obviously, I was the liar, but I didn't want to admit it to myself. I was ashamed. I was also too wrapped up in my own self right now. I was finally in position to move forward in life.

As I rolled back into the house and turned to close the door, I got a glimpse of Shane for the final time. He stood outside the door totally lost as he looked up and down the street, wondering where he would go or what he would do. I felt for him. Lord knows I did.

A part of me wanted to tell him to come back inside, but the other side of me wouldn't. I hated a snitch. As Shane returned his attention back to me, he had the most pathetic look on his face I'd ever seen. Unable to take it, I simply closed the door in his face so hard the entire house shook.

For several minutes, I sat there quiet. My conscience wouldn't let me move. All I could do was think about Shane. I even thought about his father, Dupree. Damn, I knew I was wrong. I knew I should've been ashamed of myself, but I couldn't help it. From here on out, I was gonna get what I wanted. And right now I wanted to walk; plain and simple. That was all that mattered to me. Fuck feelings. Fuck love. Fuck family. Fuck everything. If it was compromising my chance to walk again, I didn't want it anywhere near me, let alone living in my house.

All of a sudden, there was a knock on the door. Figuring

it was Shane, I ignored it. Seconds later, someone knocked again.

Why won't he just go away, I thought to myself. Another knock came. Pissed off, I grabbed the doorknob and snatched the door open. "Nigga, just go..."

To my surprise, it wasn't Shane at all. It was Ms. Kyle and Deniro. My outburst made them look at me strangely. For a moment, I didn't know what to say.

"Is everything okay?" Ms. Kyle asked.

"Uh, uh, yeah, sure, everything's good. Come in."

As I wheeled backwards, the two of them walked inside. I then closed the door and looked at Deniro. God, I felt so proud of my decision to let him move away. He looked happy.

"Boy, look at you," I told him. "You're getting bigger every time I see you."

"I missed you, mommy," he said, hugging me.

The hug was the tightest he'd ever given me. It was the tightest *anyone* had ever given me. It made me squeeze him just as tightly and close my eyes, never wanting to let him go.

"I hope you don't mind us showing up unexpectedly," Ms. Kyle said. "I've been trying to reach you. I've been texting and calling, but didn't get an answer."

"We were worried about you," Deniro chimed in. "I've been having nightmares about someone hurting you."

Kissing him on his cheek and giving him an assuring smile, I said, "Baby, I'm good. No one has tried to hurt me."

"Why haven't you been answering your phone?" Ms. Kyle inquired.

"I'm sorry, Ms. Kyle. Things have been so hectic lately. I've been making so many moves. I was going to call you, though."

Ms. Kyle only looked at me. It wasn't a disapproving look, but it was definitely a look that made me uneasy. I immediately wanted to change the subject. "Guess what?" I asked excitedly.

Deniro smiled. "What, mommy?"

"I'm going to walk again!"

Both of their mouths dropped.

"I know it sounds crazy, but I found this amazing doctor over in the Dominican Republic, and he's gonna make it all happen. Of course it's gonna take some time to get it all done, but it'll be worth it in the end."

They both continued to stare for a while.

Ms. Kyle cleared her throat. "Well, that's wonderful Keema. I'm so happy for you."

"Me, too," Deniro chimed in.

I grinned. "Thank you. I'm pretty excited."

"I hate to say this, but that sounds very expensive. Are you sure you can afford this?" Ms. Kyle questioned.

"My new boyfriend is paying for it," I lied. "He's wonderful, Ms. Kyle. I don't know what I'd do without him."

She shook her head. "Oh…well, when can I get to meet him?"

"Oh, he's away at work," I responded. "He uh, uh, he drives trucks. He makes deliveries all over the country. Right now he's in Texas."

Ms. Kyle smiled, but it wasn't one of those genuine smiles. It was like only a half of a smile. Since I wasn't sure if she believed me, I decided to paint shit on a little thicker.

"Did you see my new van outside?"

She nodded.

"He bought it for me. Ms. Kyle, he treats me like a queen."

"Where's Treasure, mommy?" Deniro asked.

"She's out with her friends."

"Can you call her? She hasn't been answering my calls. I wanna talk to her."

I could tell he missed his sister.

"Uh…uh…" I stuttered. "I'll call her in a minute."

Ms. Kyle looked at me closely. "Are you sure everything

is okay?" The slight smile she had faded. She didn't look truly convinced.

"Of course. Why do you ask?"

"Because we just saw Shane sitting on the curb crying. When I asked him what was wrong, he ignored me, got up and walked away."

I was at a loss for words. I didn't have a lie prepared.

"Yeah, why was Shane crying?" Deniro seemed concerned.

All eyes were on me.

Suddenly, Maya's son walked out of Shane's bedroom and headed towards the kitchen. My stomach dropped to my feet.

"Hi, sweetie," Ms. Kyle said, stopping him in his tracks. With a big smile she said, "Come here."

My mind scrambled for a reason why he was there.

"You're so cute," Ms. Kyle told him as she took Jaden into her arms. "What's your name?"

Jaden didn't answer. He simply glanced from her to me, scared to open his mouth.

"Are you shy?" she asked.

He kept his eyes on me.

"Who is that, Ma?" Deniro asked with a confused expression.

Once again, all eyes were on me. I didn't know what to say. All I could think about at the moment was Jaden possibly telling Ms. Kyle about his mother. I was afraid my cover was about to be blown. All of a sudden, there was another knock at the door. Thankful for a way out, no matter how temporary, I hurriedly turned and headed to the door. When I opened it, I was shocked to see two men standing there. Their faces sent chills down my spine.

"Ms. Keema Newell," one of them said.

I didn't quite know how to react. The men were the two guys I'd sold the bricks to at the carwash the day before and several days before that. Behind them were several other men dressed in jeans and T-shirts. Badges dangled from their necks. Each of them had their hands on their holstered guns.

I looked at the white guy with the disgusting pimples before finally asking, "What the hell are y'all doing here? How did you find out where I lived?"

Both men reached into their pockets, pulled out badges and flashed them. "FBI," they said in unison.

I wanted to pass out. I was light-headed at the sound of those words. The transactions flashed in my mind. The fact that I was on probation flashed. Me claiming that I was running the show while Rocco was no longer in the picture flashed, too. If I wasn't in a wheelchair, I would've turned and ran as fast as I could. Damn, these legs needed to work.

"What do you want?" I asked nervously.

"I'm pretty sure you know what it involves." The black guy who was normally the driver and had fuzzy braids, cleaned up well.

"Keema, is everything alright?" Ms. Kyle asked.

"Uh…"

I didn't know what to tell her.

"Let me take the kids in the bedroom," she told me. She then ushered both Deniro and Jaden off.

"Am I being arrested?" I asked, turning back to the agents.

They stared at me for a moment without saying a word. Sweat began to run down my back.

"Are there any drugs in the house, Ms. Newell?" the white guy inquired.

"No."

"Guns?"

"No."

"Money?"

I paused for a moment. I still had the money I'd made from all Rocco's drops. I'd called him several times this morning to find out when we were gonna hook up, but he hadn't answered. I also had the money me and Snake had split from robbing Frenchie and Shy last night. After popping them both, Snake ransacked the room until he found a Louis Vuitton duffle bag filled with forty thousand dollars. I kept twenty and Snake kept the other twenty.

"Money, Ms. Newell? Is there money in this residence?" the white guy asked, interrupting my thoughts.

"No," I lied.

They looked at me in silence.

I should've asked for a lawyer, but I froze. I was scared to death.

"Ms. Newell, we're not going to beat around the bush with you. You know exactly why we're here. We've got you on video making countless drug transactions, including some that involved both my partner and I. Each transaction involved *heavy* amounts of heroin," the white guy stated.

I wanted to cry.

"You're looking at a whole lot of time. No less than decades in prison," the black guy included.

Panic began to set in.

"Now, how much time you do is totally up to you."

I looked at the black guy. "What do you mean?"

"I'm pretty sure you already know."

We were all silent.

Of course I knew what they wanted. They wanted me to snitch.

The white guy rubbed one of the pimples with his index finger. "That's your only way out of this, Ms. Newell."

Obviously, I had a lot to tell them, if I decided to snitch. I could tell them Rocco was the boss. I could tell them about him and Snake's involvement in Mr. Evans' murder. I could tell them where Rocco's stash houses were. There was so much I could give them.

"I'll tell you what, Ms. Newell. We'll give you an hour

to think about it. That's it. When we come back, we will have a search warrant, and I guarantee you will be leaving out of here and in cuffs."

Within seconds, both agents turned around and headed out of the door. Once I looked outside and saw two different agents jump into a black Mustang GT, it was at that moment when I knew they were definitely following me. As soon as they all pulled off, I closed the door and released a huge breath I didn't even known I'd been holding. I had no idea what to do. I'd come so close to walking again. It was on the verge of reality. All I had to do was hop on that plane. Now, shit had suddenly gotten complicated. I was looking at time in prison. I'd never walk again if that happened. It was then I realized I had no choice. Fuck Rocco. Whatever the agents needed from me, I was going to give them. Afterwards, I was going to hop on that plane to the Dominican Republic and never come back.

Ms. Kyle came out of the room. Seeing the stress written on my face, she asked, "Keema, what's going on?"

Suddenly, the kids came out of the bedroom and looked at me, too.

Someone knocked at the door. Thinking it was the agents coming back already, I opened the door ready to cooperate. Instead of the agents though, it was Toy, Shane and two other girls.

"Toy, where the hell have you been? Look, you need to get that little boy, now!" I shouted. "And what the fuck happened to you? You never showed up at the hotel!"

Before I could say anything else, one of the girls shoved Shane inside while Toy smirked; snidely expressing that she was in on the shit. That's when I saw the guns in their hands.

"Oh God!" Ms. Kyle said fearfully as she backed up and placed herself in front of the kids.

"Toy, what the hell is going on?" I asked. "What do y'all want?"

"You know what the fuck we want. We want that tramp

ass daughter of yours," one of the girls responded.

"Well, she's not here." I glanced at Toy. "You better handle these damn girls, and why did you bring them to my house? Whatever beef y'all got with Treasure needs to be dealt with her."

Suddenly, all three of the girls looked at Ms. Kyle and the kids.

"Please," Ms. Kyle begged, staying tightly in front of Deniro and Jaden. "The kids have nothing to do with this."

The tallest girl glared at me. "Where's Treasure?"

I shook my head. "I don't know."

"She's lying, Tangie," Toy instigated.

They both cocked their guns. The sound made my heart rise up into my throat.

Ms. Kyle grabbed the kids and they began to cry.

"Shoot one and they'll all start talking," Toy suggested. "I guarantee it."

Seeing tears fall from Deniro's eyes broke my heart. Once again, my selfishness had placed my flesh and blood in harm's way. When was I going to learn? Once again, I was getting ready to lose a baby to a bullet that was meant for me. I couldn't bear it.

Ms. Kyle had the children in her arms, but in a way that would ensure she'd be shot first if the girl's pulled the trigger. She'd put her life on the line for two children who weren't even hers. The sight made me ashamed of myself. She had more heart and love than I did. I admired her for that.

The lies flooded my head. The murders flooded my thoughts. My selfishness and inconsideration flashed in front of my eyes. I had to admit that I'd been a terrible mother. I'd lost one child and my only daughter hated me. I realized the cycle had to be stopped. I deserved whatever was coming to me. My children didn't.

"Look," I pleaded. "They have nothing to do with this. Leave them out of this."

The taller girl, Tangie smirked. "Why the fuck should we?"

"Because I'll pay you. I've got money."

Both girls, including Toy looked at me.

"It's in my bedroom. I swear. There's jewelry, too."

I was willing to give them all the money that belonged to Rocco along with the money me and Snake stole from Frenchie and Shy. The jewelry was Treasure's. I was willing to give it all up for my baby's life, the life of a good friend, and the life of a child who'd already seen his mother brutally murdered.

"Where at in your bedroom?" the other girl questioned.

"Underneath my bed. The jewelry is in the room across from mine," I informed her.

"I know where it is, Destiny," Toy said as she led the girl to the rooms while Tangie kept her gun on me.

Moments later, Toy and Destiny appeared with the bag of money and Treasure's jewelry. All of the girls smiled at each other.

"Alright, bitch," Tangie told me. "Let's go."

"Leave Keema alone!" Shane suddenly blurted out.

"Where are we going? Where are you taking me?" I asked them.

"On a ride you won't be comin' back from. That's all you need to know," Tangie replied.

Deniro tried to break free from Ms. Kyle, but she refused to let him go. Tears filled my own eyes as I realized this was the very last time I would see his face. My heart was broken into a million pieces. I saw the day I gave birth to him. I saw the day he took his first steps. I saw the day he spoke his first words. Each of those moments was just as vivid as the day they happened. I wished with all my heart I could get them back.

The girls escorted me to the door.

"Keema!" Ms. Kyle called.

I turned to her.

"Pray, child," she told me with sad eyes. "Pray and keep your faith. God is going to keep you safe."

I gave her a peaceful smile. Her words were comforting, but I knew there was no need in holding onto hope. I knew what the girl said was true…

This was a ride from which I would not return.

Chapter 23-
Treasure

I pulled up to Rasheeda's house and quickly hopped out. Glancing around and not seeing her car or her mother's, I jogged up the front steps, snatched open the screen door and began to bang...hard. While waiting for someone to answer, I anxiously glanced up and down the street and patted my foot on the ground; unable to stand totally still. I was in an absolute rush. After only a few seconds of waiting with no answer, I banged again, this time harder.

"Rasheeda, I know you're up in here!" I yelled. "Open this damn door up. I want my damn money, bitch!"

After several more seconds of not getting an answer, I let the screen door slam as I headed down the stairs and began to make my way to the backyard, peeking through a few windows along the way. All the blinds were down, so I couldn't see anything inside.

"Rasheeda, you can't hide forever, tramp!" I yelled as I made my way back towards the front. "I know you're up in there!"

Once again, I was back at the front door pounding like

the police.

"You're not gonna get an answer," a voice suddenly said.

I turned to see the next door neighbor peeking out of her door at me. She was an older lady, who was extremely nosey.

"Why not?"

"Because no one lives there anymore."

I panicked, my breathing getting shallow as I looked at her with deep concern. "What do you mean by that?"

"I mean no one lives there anymore. They moved out."

I walked towards her, needing to be sure I'd heard her correctly. "They moved?"

She nodded.

"When?"

"This morning."

"How do you know that?"

"Because they had the U-Haul truck out there. It took them about three or four hours."

"Are you sure?"

She nodded again. "I know a U-Haul truck when I see one, sweetheart."

I was in complete disbelief. "Well, did they say where they were moving to?"

"Nope."

I stood there for a minute taking it all in.

"Well, I've gotta get back in here and finish watching Ellen. I just wanted to come out and let you know you were wasting your time doing all that beating and yelling."

She closed her door.

"That lowdown bitch!" I screamed. Rasheeda knew I would come after her, so she didn't waste much time getting the hell out of town. I was pissed at myself for letting the bitch get over on me.

After cursing myself out a few more seconds, I climbed back into my car, backed out of the driveway and drove off at a dangerous speed. I felt betrayed by everyone. Toy, Rasheeda, my mother…even Rocco. I was infuriated beyond words at what Shane had told me. As a matter of fact, I didn't know who's head I wanted most; his or my mother's.

Both totally shocked me. Of course, I knew my mother was a sneaky bitch and couldn't be trusted. But never in a million years would I have imagined that she'd fuck my man. That was just unbelievable. I would've never seen it coming. But at the same time, I never imagined Rocco would be the type of nigga to fuck around with my own mother, either. Shit, I expected him to fuck with other bitches. But my damn crippled ass mother? I knew the perfect way to get her back though. One call to her probation officer and she would be fucked.

Right now, I was headed to meet Rocco's unfaithful, lying ass. Once I called and told him we needed to talk, I failed to mention that I knew anything about him and my mother. I hadn't mentioned it at all. Holding my tongue was the hardest thing I'd ever done. Once upon a time, his voice, face and touch use to make my pussy soaking wet. Now, I needed time to avoid his voice and face. I needed time to avoid his touch. Never in my lifetime did I think I would ever hate him. Now, I did.

I wasn't quite sure what was ahead for me and Rocco. I was pissed and my heart was broken because I loved him. But despite the love, letting him get away with doing the ultimate betrayal was not an option. Somehow he had to pay.

Among all the emotions, I was also preoccupied with Frenchie and Shy's duffle bag back at the hotel. My attraction to money was like that. I couldn't help it. I wanted that bag. I needed that bag, especially after taking such a huge loss from Rasheeda. Someone had to pay. And it looked like it was going to be Frenchie and Shy.

Almost thirty minutes later, I pulled into the lot of Broadway Diner on Eastern Avenue, parked and headed inside. When Rocco and I made eye contact, he stood from his table and greeted me with a smile and open arms, expecting a damn hug. I couldn't take it. I used to love being held inside those arms.

Not now though.

Unable to hold back, I smacked the shit out of him so hard the sound of my hand connecting with his face echoed across the diner. Everyone went silent and stared at us.

He held his face, then looked at me with wide eyes. "Treasure, what the fuck is wrong with you? Are you crazy?"

"My mother, Rocco?"

"What?"

"You let my mother suck your dick?"

He swiftly glanced around the diner. "Lower your voice. What are you talkin' about?"

His response seemed genuine. He honestly looked like he didn't know what I was talking about.

"You know what I'm talking about, Rocco. Don't play stupid. That's why you gave her a job, huh? That's why you've been treating her special lately? Is the head that good?"

After sitting back down, Rocco looked at me like what I was saying was disgusting. "Where did you hear some shit like that, Treasure? Who told you that?"

I sat down across from him. "Shane."

He mustered a small smile. "Shane? Are you serious? You're gonna believe that retarded muthafucka. He's lyin'."

"Shane wouldn't lie about something like that. He may be a little slow, but he *always* repeats what he sees."

Looking directly into my eyes with a sincere seriousness, he said, "Baby, I didn't do what you're accusin' me of."

His eyes and tone began to break me down.

"I swear, baby, I would never hurt you, especially by doin' somethin' *that* damn foul. I swear to God."

His tone was soft and calm.

"But, baby," I said with my words now sounding more like a whiny pout. "Why would Shane say something like that?"

Rocco shrugged his shoulders. "I don't know. I really

don't."

Damn, I believed him.

As I watched Rocco and listened to his words, my eyes glanced over his shoulder to a flat screen television on the wall. Suddenly, Kendrick's face appeared. He was being hauled out of his church in handcuffs by the police while the caption at the bottom read, *Local pastor arrested for having sex with an underaged minor*. I wanted to jump for joy. It was the first thing that had gone right. I shook my leg with excitement, trying not to let Rocco know what was going on.

"Baby, don't let this shit break us up," I managed to hear Rocco say as my attention finally drifted back to him from the television.

I eventually got up, sat beside him, then planted a kiss on his lips. Inside though, I was torn. I didn't quite know whether to believe him or not. Shane had never lied about anything, especially something this serious. But there was a first time for everything. He could've possibly been jealous that I no longer had time for him since I was now hustling hard and spending a lot of time with Rocco. I wasn't sure.

"You hungry?" Rocco asked. He already had a bacon cheeseburger in front of him.

"Nah," I told him. With all the stress that had fallen on my shoulders lately, I didn't have an appetite.

"You sure?"

"Yeah."

He took a sip of his Coke, glanced at his watch and said, "Ole boy should be here soon."

"Who?" I didn't know we were having company.

"One of my associates."

"About what?"

"Nothin' too important."

"Well, who is he?"

"Somebody I've been fuckin' with lately."

I hated when he talked like that. He never gave me full

answers. They were always short and clipped like he didn't want to divulge too much information to me. Damn, the two of us had so many secrets between us.

While sitting there, I remembered the girl Brianna from school giving me her phone number. I'd meant to call her, but totally forgot. As I reached into my purse to make sure the number was still in there, a white guy with terrible acne walked up to our table. Rocco offered him a seat.

He looked at me and then back at Rocco. "Who is she?"

"She's good. Don't worry about it," Rocco tried to convince.

The man appeared worried. "You sure?"

"Yeah. So, how did shit turn out?"

The white guy smirked. "Exactly as planned."

Rocco smiled, too.

I had no idea what they were talking about.

"We've got video of her saying she's calling all the shots, not *you*," the man continued. We've got her making transactions. We've got it all, everything we need to bury her with some real charges and real prison time."

"You sure?" Rocco questioned.

"Trust me; we got her."

"No problems that'll come back to haunt me later?"

The guy shook his head. "None."

Rocco looked at him skeptically.

"Trust me, Rocco, it'll fly," the guy replied confidently.

"Shit, for fifty grand it better."

"Speaking of payments, we'll need to switch up our hook up spots. I don't like being in one spot more than twice. Of course the department doesn't know anything about this, and I don't want to do anything that could possibly draw attention," the guy informed.

At that moment, I got a gut wrenching feeling that they might've been talking about my mother, but I wasn't a hundred percent sure. If they were, that meant this white guy was a fucking informant. That also meant that Rocco was in on it.

I gazed at Rocco, hoping my assumption wasn't true as he nodded.

After a few more words, the white guy got up and left.

"What was all that about?"

Before Rocco could give me an answer, his cell phone rang. "What up, Snake?"

"The Frenchie nigga and that bitch are dead," Snake informed.

The volume on Rocco's phone was loud enough for me to hear the conversation. I was shocked to hear the news. Rocco was, too.

"What the hell do you mean, *dead*?" Rooco asked.

I leaned in a little closer, so I could hear clearly.

"I mean, dead. There aren't too many ways to put it. I mean tag on your big toe, body stuffed in a zipped black bag, *dead*."

"Don't play with me, Snake. I'm not in the mood for jokes. You were supposed to be watchin' them. How did that shit happen?"

"I don't know, bruh. I left for a minute to go get somethin' to eat since your ass didn't come back to check on me. When I came back, the damn police were at the hotel. They were posted up all around the Range. Next thing I know, I saw two muthafukas comin' out in body bags."

"But how did you know it was them?" Rocco inquired.

"Cuz, the police eventually towed the Range away. It had to be them," Snake replied.

"That shit doesn't make any sense, Snake. Yo,' keep yo' phone close to you. I'm gonna hit you back."

With that said, Rocco hung up.

"Let's go," Rocco said plainly. He tossed a twenty dollar bill on the table for the waitress and stood up.

"Rocco, what's going on? Where are we going?"

"Just come the fuck on, Treasure!"

He turned and headed straight for the door, leaving me surprised at how he'd just spoken. Since we'd been together, he'd never spoken to me like that. I wanted to snap, but followed him outside; curious to know what exactly had happened to Frenchie and Shy. Rocco was right, Snake's story didn't make sense at all.

"Am I taking my car?"

"Nah, you ridin' with me."

His tone was still harsh.

The two of us got into his car. However, before I could react or ask anymore questions, Rocco pulled a gun from his waist and placed it directly against my temple.

My eyes enlarged. "Rocco, what the hell are you doing?"

"Shut the fuck up!" he ordered.

Looking at him now was like looking at a stranger. I didn't recognize him. He'd switched up like Doctor Jekyll and Mr. Hyde and I didn't have the slightest reason why.

"Baby," I pleaded. "What did I do?"

"Fuck that *baby* shit!" He grabbed a roll of duct tape from the backseat and tossed it in my lap. "Tape up your ankles."

Tears starting running down my face out of fear and frustration. "Why…why are you doing this? Baby, just talk to…"

The sound of Rocco's hand striking my face echoed throughout the car. The force was so hard it immediately made my ears ring.

"Do it, bitch!"

As confused as I was, I had no choice but to do as I was told. When I was done, he taped my wrists. Tears continued to fall from my eyes, frantically.

"What did I do?" I pleaded. "Baby, whatever it is, I'm sorry."

"For what you did, there is no sorry," Rocco coldly responded.

I had no idea what I'd done or what he was talking about.

"What did you think my tattoo stood for?"

I was so confused. "What?"

"It meant I'd lost someone close to me, someone I loved more than life itself."

"But what does that have to do with why you're doing this to me?"

"It has *everything* to do with it!" he yelled. "You and your mother are the reason I have this tattoo." He tapped his chest with force.

I was completely clueless.

He finally started the car and said, "Now, it's payback time. Time for you to meet your damn maker."

"Rocco, oh God, I'm sorry."

"No need. It's time for you to die."

"Whatever you're mad at me for…"

He taped my mouth shut.

As we pulled away from the diner, all I could think about was how things were supposed to be. We were supposed to get married. We were supposed to have kids. I was supposed to spend the rest of my life with him. Now, the man I loved was going to kill me and I had no idea why.

Chapter 24-

Keema

My head ached badly. Blood ran down the side of my face. The vision in my left eye was blurry and my bottom lip was both split and swollen. I wanted to cry, but realized there was no use. Tears wouldn't change anything.

The long stretch of road ahead of me was dark and desolate. It was lined with fields and trees. I hadn't seen another car or even a person for the past couple of miles. We were truly on the outskirts of Baltimore in no man's land and it seemed like I'd been driving forever. Most people who got kidnapped in movies didn't have to drive themselves to the secret location. Lazy bitches.

As I drove, I could feel Toy's eyes on me from the passenger seat. "I'll bet when you woke up this mornin', you had no idea you'd be dyin' today, huh?" she asked with a snicker as she held her gun on me.

"Fuck you," I told her while keeping my eyes on the road.

She laughed.

"I trusted you, Toy," I added.

"I know. That's why the shit was so easy."

"Sneaky bitch." I wanted to spit in her face.

"Look who's callin' the kettle black. You and Treasure are about as sneaky as they come."

She was right about that one.

"I'm just givin' you back what you gave out. Besides, if it wasn't me who set you up, it would've been someone else. So shit, why not go ahead and get the money. Tangie and Destiny paid me to turn on your ass? Why let someone else receive that payday?"

"Fuck you," I repeated.

She chuckled. "Awww, Keema, don't act like that. It's business, that's all. It's not personal."

"Turn right here," Tangie said from the back seat.

I turned right onto a dirt road. Just like the stretch of road I was leaving behind, there didn't seem to be a living soul in sight. There were no houses or even street lamps. The only illumination came from my van's headlights. After several minutes, I finally saw something ahead on the left hand side. I couldn't make it out at first. But as I got closer, I realized it was an old cemetery.

"Slow down," Tangie ordered.

I eased off the gas pedal.

As we approached the cemetery's entrance, she said, "Pull inside."

Immediately, my heartbeat began to speed up as I turned and entered underneath the old arched entrance. What the fuck was in the cemetery? Why were they bringing me there? Sweat began pouring down my face as I watched head stone after head stone pass by my window. Finally, ahead of me I saw something I couldn't make out at first. As I got closer, I realized it was an SUV.

"Pull behind the truck," Destiny stated. I could already tell that she was the quieter one out of the crew. She didn't talk much.

I did as I was told.

"You're gonna love what we've got planned for you," Toy said with a smile on her face.

Moments later, we were out of the van and I was being shoved into my wheelchair.

"Roll, bitch," Tangie ordered.

"It's not easy rolling over rocks and shit in case you haven't noticed!" I fired back.

As the four of us headed into the cemetery's darkness, I saw what looked like a flashlight ahead of us. The closer we got, I finally saw who was holding the flashlight. It was Rocco. In front of him was both Snake and Treasure who were digging separate holes with shovels.

What the fuck is going on, I wondered.

How did the girls who'd kidnapped me know Rocco? But the even more puzzling question was, what was Treasure and Snake doing here?

When we approached them, I could hear Treasure whimpering. Tears strolled down her face at a rapid pace, and her hair was a mess. Her clothes were also dirty and sweaty. Apparently, she'd been digging for a while.

"Treasure, are you okay?" I asked, worried about her.

Treasure looked at me pitifully. For a moment, she stopped digging.

"Bitch, did I tell you to stop?" Rocco questioned.

It looked as if Treasure didn't have one ounce of energy for a comeback. Instead, she went back to digging.

"And stop all that damn cryin'," Tangie ordered. "Soldiers don't cry. You knew death was comin' your way. Now dig, or get your head splattered."

I noticed Rocco had a gun tucked in his pants. This shit didn't make any sense to me.

I looked at him. "Rocco, what's going on?"

He looked at me with a sneer. It was an expression I'd

never seen on his face before. He looked like a stranger. "So, I see you met my sisters, huh?" he asked.

"Sisters?" I was confused.

Even Treasure stopped digging for a second and looked up with a shocked expression.

"Rocco, what is this all about?"

"Revenge," he replied to me. "It's that plain and simple."

"Revenge for what? I never crossed you. I never did anything to you," I quickly responded.

"You sure about that?" Destiny asked.

"Yes, I'm sure," I snapped.

"The bitch has the blood of our dead father on her hands, but has the nerve to say she never crossed us," Tangie commented.

"Your father?" Once again I was puzzled. "What are you talking about?"

"You should've never come back to Baltimore, Keema," Rocco stated. "You should've stayed away."

I had no idea what was going on. I had no idea who their father was.

"Rocco, who is your father? What are you talking about?"

Rocco stepped closer to me. "Look into my face, bitch." I did.

"See anything familiar?" His face held so much hate.

"Rocco I..."

"Look hard!" he screamed. Specks of spit flew onto my nose.

I surveyed every inch of his face, every curve. Within seconds, I saw something familiar. I saw the familiarity of someone I'd known in the past. My mouth opened slightly in surprise.

"Yeah, it's as plain as day, ain't it?" Rocco asked.

I couldn't believe how obvious it was. I couldn't believe

I'd never noticed it before now. "Oh my, God," I whispered in absolute shock.

In my mind, I could still hear that frightful gunshot from long ago. I saw the dead body. I saw the blood pouring from his chest. It was as if it happened only seconds ago, although it was a memory I'd put out of my mind years ago. I'd forgotten about it. But forgetting it didn't change anything. It didn't change the fact that Rocco's father was dead. That day back in Arizona was one that I'd never forget.

"Paco was your father?" I asked in complete disbelief.

"Yes!" Tangie yelled out.

I was speechless at that point. I could only sit there with my mouth open.

"Rocco, I had nothing to do with your father's death," Treasure suddenly pleaded. "It was my mother who crossed you. Please don't do this to me. I love you."

"Shut the fuck up!" Tangie shouted. "Keep diggin'!"

"But, Rocco, baby, you know I love you," Treasure sobbed.

Rocco turned and faced her. It was obvious he had feelings for her, but his yearning for revenge had its claws dug deeply into his flesh. He was struggling with his feelings at that moment.

"It was my mother who did this to you, not me," Treasure said once again.

The bitch was throwing me all the way under the bus. "You lying bitch," I sneered. "Shane was the one who pulled the trigger. Rocco, I swear it was Shane who did it. He's the one who you really want. As a matter of fact, Shane is back at my place right now. I can go get him if you want."

I was already preparing to put my wheelchair in gear.

"Nah, bitch," Tangie responded. "We got who we want. You're not goin' any muthafuckin' where."

"Rocco," Treasure continued to plead.

"Dig!" he snapped at her.

"But my leg hurts so bad," she cried.

It was then that I noticed the bullet hole in her thigh. Blood was all over her pants.

"Dig!" Toy finally chimed in.

Rocco turned and looked at Toy. "Shut the fuck up! Nobody asked for your input. I know you told my sisters where to find Keema, but they shouldn't have brought your ass out here."

Treasure had no choice but to do what she was told. As she began to dig again, she looked at me with both sadness and spite. She hated me with all her being. I hated that it had all come to this, but there was no changing it. It was now every bitch for herself.

"Alright, Snake," Rocco said. "Your hole is deep enough."

Snake stopped digging and dropped his shovel.

For several minutes, we all watched as Treasure continued to dig. Watching was the scariest thing I'd ever seen. There's nothing like the terror of witnessing your own grave being dug. As I gazed at her, I could picture the worms and maggots feasting on my dead body. The thought horrified me.

"Alright, that's good enough," Rocco finally told her.

Treasure stopped and wiped her forehead with her arm.

My heart pounded harder and faster than before as if that were possible. I knew I was only seconds away from death.

"Get over here," Rocco ordered Treasure.

"Baby, don't do this," she pleaded, scared to go near him.

"Bitch, you heard my damn brother!" Tangie yelled. She walked over, grabbed Treasure by the arm, then shoved her. "Get over there!"

Treasure fell to Rocco's feet. "Don't do this," she begged. "I'll do anything you want. I swear I will." The words tumbled from her mouth.

"Get on your knees," he ordered.

"But…" Treasure attempted to say.

"Get on your fuckin' knees, now!" Rocco roared.

Treasure reluctantly did as she was told. Rocco then placed the tip of his gun against the center of her forehead. She looked up at him with pain and sadness in her eyes.

"Baby," she whispered. "I love you. You know I do. And you know you love me. We can make this right. There can still be an us."

Rocco didn't say anything. He just stared down into her tear filled eyes, continuing to keep the gun aimed.

It was then that Snake walked over to me. He hadn't said a word since I'd gotten there. He hadn't even given me any eye contact until now. He pulled his gun from behind his back and cocked it. At that moment, reality hit me like a ton of bricks. I knew I was literally staring at death.

"Snake, don't do this," I begged.

He didn't reply. He just aimed at my head.

"Snake, we're partners. Please don't kill me," I said.

Snake still said nothing. His stare was as hard as stone.

Seeing that I didn't' have any luck with Snake, I turned my pleading to Rocco. "Rocco, please let me go. If you let me go, I'll disappear. I swear I will. You'll never see me again. I'll go somewhere far away."

As I spoke, knowing my life literally depended on it, Treasure remained on her knees. She'd now dropped her head down. "Oh God, I don't want to die," she began to repeat over and over.

"God ain't here for you," Destiny told her.

"Rocco, have mercy on us," I said. My vision was blurry as tears fell from my eyes.

"Have mercy?" Tangie repeated like it was an outrageous request. "Have mercy? Did you have mercy when you killed our father? Did you show him any mercy?"

"But he was gonna kill me. I swear he was. I had no choice," I tried to convince.

"Fuck that!" Rocco cocked his gun, ready to now send

Treasure to Heaven or Hell; whichever one was waiting for her.

"Murk her ass," Tangie urged him.

I hated to see Treasure's life end this way, but in all honesty, I was too worried about my own life to give her circumstances any thought. My plate was already full.

"Snake, don't kill me," I begged. My eyes repeatedly glanced from the gun to his face.

"Kill 'em both," Tangie kept urging.

Toy wasn't saying anything, but she watched, never letting her eyes leave the action even for a brief second.

All of a sudden, I watched as Rocco walked over towards me. My eyes widened with fear, wondering what he was about to do. Did he decide to kill me first instead of Treasure? All types of thoughts rapidly circulated through my head. I didn't know what to do. My body shook uncontrollably as Rocco stopped within inches of me. He slowly raised his gun and placed his finger around the trigger. I closed my eyes, ready for my fate. But when the gun went off, I heard a loud thump hit the ground. Once I opened them and looked around, I saw Snake's body lying in a pool of bright red blood. He'd been shot directly in his chest.

At that moment, I looked at Treasure hoping that she would try to save me like she always did. But surprisingly, she just sat there. This time her eyes were cold; like she was tired of fighting for me; like I deserved whatever was about to come my way. It looked like she didn't love me anymore.

I didn't even get a chance to cry out before Tangie swiftly walked over to me and placed the gun against my temple.

CRACK!!!

When her gun went off, I felt the bullet tear through my head. The force was so powerful it knocked me backwards and out of my chair and onto the ground. Seconds later, six other bullets tore through what was left of my frail body. At that moment, everything went black.

Epilogue–

Treasure
Two Years Later

Still Breathing.

For now anyway.

Yes, that grave two years ago was dug for me. One for my mother and one for me. Yet, somehow, love won over hate. Rocco could've killed me as he'd planned. He could've taken my life as payback for being associated with someone who'd hurt him and his family. But I guess his heart wouldn't allow him to do it. He turned the gun on Snake instead.

I didn't find out the reason why he'd killed Snake until weeks later when we fled the city of Baltimore together. Although Rocco didn't talk about it much, he clearly stated that he didn't want any disloyal men in his army. By Toy telling him that my mother paid Snake to kill Frenchie, and by Snake lying about it, Rocco felt betrayed by his own right hand man. If Snake was capable of that, he was capable of anything, so it was only right that Rocco got rid of that situation.

The crazy thing is, he didn't get rid of me, too. His love for me had triumphed over everything: money, deceit, grinding, history, my mother and his sisters. They damn near wanted to kill me themselves when they realized Rocco wasn't going to end my life. Tangie even suggested that he bury me alive in the same grave my mother's body had been thrown into.

None of that happened, of course. Instead, Rocco took me into his arms and hugged me tightly right there in the cemetery; telling me that he just couldn't do it; telling me that he was in love and couldn't bring himself to let me go. I guess we had that Chris Brown and Rihanna shit going on. Nonetheless, the relationship with Rocco and his sisters ended that day. Because of his choice, they refused to deal with him after that; dissolving any relationship they once had. They never call or even know where we live. They probably have no clue that our now permanent residence is Atlanta. They've never even met the newest addition to our family, Marley, my three-month-old baby boy.

Sadly, when I look into his eyes, he reminds me so much of my mother and Cash. But the day I gave birth, I vowed to never let him experience any of the pain my family left behind. I was extremely overprotective of him. I was even more protective of Shane, Deniro and Ms. Kyle who all live in one big house down the street from mine. I even convinced Lucky and his wife to move to Georgia with us. Sometimes when I look at Deniro playing with my son, I often think about Maya's son, Jaden and wonder how he's adjusted since his mother passed away.

As a mother now, I felt bad about the pain I'd placed in his life that day and often regret my decision. A week or two after everything went down, Ms. Kyle eventually found Maya's mother in Columbia, MD, who gladly took her grandson in with open arms. At first I thought it was a bad idea for Ms. Kyle to search for Maya's family. I knew we couldn't keep Jaden forever; acting as if he was a part of our family, but I didn't want my involvement with Maya's kidnapping to ever reach the police. I can't even express how lucky I am because as of today, the police have yet to knock on my door about that.

However, I can't say the same for Toy.

As soon as Jaden was reunited with his family, he obviously didn't waste any time telling the police about his mother's murder, and the name of the girl responsible for killing her. Eventually, it didn't take long for the police to catch up with Toy and she was ultimately charged for Maya's murder. Months after I left Baltimore, I found out that she was tried, convicted, and sentenced to life without parole.

Once again, I'd dodged another bullet, which has a lot to do with me turning my life around. At times, it's been hard for me to forgive myself for the mistakes of my misguided past. But I found out that healing comes from letting go and moving on. I've accomplished this by learning from my mistakes and not repeating them. I also decided not to let my past experiences dictate my future. In the end, I know I've done a lot of wrong, but I'm a changed person, and if it takes the rest of my life...I will become the person I should've been all along.

It's just too bad that my mother, Keema, didn't get a chance to make peace with the people she hurt and repair her wrong doings before her time expired. Shane missed her more than anyone, but I'm sure over time he'll learn that her death was meant to be. Now...we finally have a chance to become a functional family for once.

Rest in Peace, Ma.

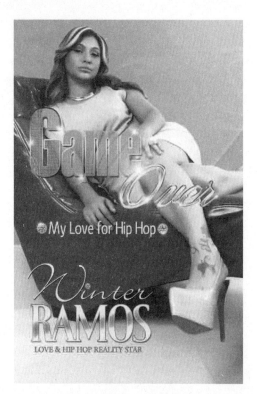

Winter Ramos, one of the new faces of VH1's hit reality television show, Love and Hip Hop New York Season 3 delivers a brazen and unabashed memoir of her life in the world of hip hop. In Game Over, Winter puts all of her emotions on the page leaving no experience, emotional abuse, or former lover uncovered. From her days as assistant to rapper, Fabolous and friend to Jada Kiss, to appearing on Love and Hip Hop and being Creative Costume Designer for Flavor unit Films, Winter delivers a tell-all book on her famous ex-lovers and experiences in the music industry. As the chick that was always in the mix and cool with everyone, Winter was privy to the cray beyond the videos, private flights, and limos that the cameras caught for us. Her reality and theirs was no game. Game Over is Winter's cautionary tale for the next generation of young women who believe that the fabulous lives of celebrities unveiled in blogs and on reality television shows are all FIRE! Stay tuned, because this GAME is about to get real.

In Stores...April 1, 2013